Bagging
ALICE

LAURA BARNARD

This book is dedicated to my amazing husband Simon.

Without him this book wouldn't have got done.

His constant support, jokes and love make it easy to write love stories.

Chapter 1

Alice

God, I hate sucking cock. So many girls bullshit about loving it. How can they? Especially when you have an insensitive guy like mine who insists on grabbing hold of my head and pushing me down so far, I think I'm gonna retch.

It always starts off okay, but then your neck starts hurting and your jaw aches. Plus, there's too much to remember to do. Suck, fist, play with balls, and all while trying not to choke and looking for those tell-tale signs that he's about to come. I don't swallow. Call me a prude, but the one time I did I thought I was going to vomit. Gross.

Tonight's no exception. Ted, a guy I've been seeing for the last two months, is forcing my head down so low I'd be surprised if his cock doesn't come out of my ear soon. This is Ted all over. He's always pressuring me into doing stuff I'm not comfortable with. Like when he tried to lick my arsehole. How the hell is that supposed to be sexy? I mean do people even do that? And if they do, surely, they have to shower first and discuss their bowel movements? You wouldn't want to go down there if you had a bad curry the night before. Ugh, just imagine. I did not enjoy that at all.

He's always calling me a prude which is why I loved shocking the fuck out of him by sending him some dirty pics last week while he was away with work. He went down on me twice when he got back. Totally worth the cringey porn-esque poses I tried to pull.

He hasn't always been a total shit. He's damn hot in bed which is why I think I stay. I mean arrogant twats always are, aren't they? Plus, he's big and burly. I feel protected when I'm around him and I know he'd never let anyone hurt me. A guy once pinched my arse in a club and he tried to bottle him. Yeah, it's safe to say he's the jealous type. Possibly the psycho type too, but maybe that's what I'm into.

He rams himself into the back of my throat grunting expletives. Ugh, I'm gonna gag so hard in a minute. My stomach starts to turn on its side, repulsed by the idea of its next meal.

'Oh, babe, that's it! Take it deep!'

He thrusts again so hard that my gag reflex instinctively goes into action. Only he keeps me there gagging... I feel my stomach churn, twisting vomit up my throat and before I can say *"get your dick out of my mouth"*—which of course I can't because it's stuffed with his cock—I'm full on vomiting on him. On his penis. I chuck up so bad I see last week's carrots from my roast dinner. What the fuck?

I look up at him wide-eyed in horror. He stares back, eyes wide in repulsion. Well, this is embarrassing.

'What the fuck, Alice?'

I should apologise. Only... well, vomiting that hard because he's an impatient twat makes me feel anything but apologetic. My throat burns, and my neck is sweaty.

'It wouldn't have happened if you hadn't been trying to choke me!' I scream, like the pushed-to-the-limit woman

I currently am. 'God, why are you such an insensitive arsehole?'

The vein on his forehead throbs. 'How the fuck are you making this my fault?' He asks with barely concealed rage. 'You just threw up on my junk.'

Suddenly it dawns on me. What the hell am I doing with this tool? I'm only twenty-six and I'm acting like he's the last Neanderthal on the planet. I can do so much better. Why am I settling? Just because Erica and Brooke are all coupled up doesn't mean I need to be seeing someone.

'You know what, Ted? Fuck you. We're over.'

I stand up and grab my bag.

'I'd walk you out,' he scoffs, 'but you know,' he points bitchily to his vomit covered floppy penis.

Saturday 6th October

Alice

I stare back at the image in front of me feeling numb. No, just numb on the outside. Inside, my stomach has curled up and run the fuck off to Hawaii. How? How could he do this to me?

I look at myself naked in an embarrassing porn-esque position. I mean I'm butt ass naked. Or more like vagina naked. I mean you can see it. My tits are on show too, but women sunbathe on the beach topless, right? They hardly ever get their vagina out. And you can clearly see my face, pouting like an absolute whore. Above it is written **This whore, Alice Watts, dumped my arse after vomiting all over my dick. What a sick bitch.**

How the hell could he have done this to me? I know we broke up, but Jesus we had a good thing going for a while there. I let the guy lick my arsehole. Did that mean absolutely nothing to him?

Does he hate me that much he can't see this is horrendously spiteful? Surely, he still holds some respect for me as a human being? Or maybe vomiting on a guy while giving a blowie really does eradicate all of that.

I read the comments below it.

On your junk? What a sick whore.

Looks like she wants it hard, dirty whore.

What a skank. I'd fuck her like the whore she is.

I swallow down yet more vomit. Apparently, I'm full of it these days.

And it goes on like that. According to this, there are over five-hundred-and-fifty similar comments. I suppose that's the kind of people you attract on a website called *Revenge Porn Utopia.*

I just can't believe it's happened to me. How could I ever have been so stupid as to trust him? I close the email from Erica. So, this explains why today has been the worst of my life. Why I got sacked from my job at the children's centre photographing newborns. They said I'd disgraced the company. Why every mother I passed was staring and whispering.

Another email from Erica pops up.

Babe, it's being shared on Facebook. I keep reporting them, but people are seeing it!

This is a fucking nightmare. As we speak, people are looking at me naked. I feel violated; like I've been touched by every single person viewing it. And without my permission. This is seriously fucked up. I'm never going to be able to show my face in this town again.

I race home, needing some kind of protection from the world. I start opening my post, anything to take my mind off this for a few minutes. Bills, bills, bills.

'Babe,' my Barbie doll of a roommate Carly says carefully, approaching me with slow steps.

I force a smile at her. I can't stand the dumb cow, but without her I'd never be able to afford this place. And it's so close to the beach.

'I know it's probably a terrible time for you right now, what with your vag being on display to the world...' She's not known for her tact. Obviously seen it herself then. 'But I'm moving out.'

I stare back at her dumbfounded. Is she serious?

'I'm sorry, babe, but I think it's for the best.' She wheels out a baby pink suitcase I hadn't noticed before. She's already packed?

'How exactly is you moving out with only a day's notice for the best?' I snap, hand on hip.

'Sorry, babe. I meant the best for me and Mike.'

One thing I won't miss is the way she says babe. It's so condescending; like she thinks she's better than me. When the truth is she's an artificial blonde with fake breasts that I found myself living with after putting an ad in the local paper. And best for her and Mike? She's only been dating the I-shout-really-loud-when-I-come bloke for a few months.

'So, I'm just left to find a new roommate with no notice?'

'Look, babe. Let's not pretend we're besties or anything. Me and Mike have been annoying you these last few months. It only makes sense that I move in with him.'

I scoff. 'Sorry, I suppose I just figured you'd have some loyalty and wouldn't leave me in the lurch like this. How the hell am I going to pay next month's rent?'

She closes her suitcase. 'Sorry, babe. Your problem now.'

The bitch.

Chapter 2

Alice

'I can't believe she just left you like that,' Erica sympathises over lunch the next day.

'Yeah, don't you have a contract in place or something?' Evelyn asks, already no doubt googling my rights on her iPad.

'No,' I sigh, my shoulders slumping pathetically. 'The rent agreement is in my name. And even if I wanted to move back home, which is *obviously* a no-go, I'd still have to give them at least three months' notice because I'm tied into it.'

Eugh, just the idea of having to move home has my stomach clenching.

'Rubbish,' Molly says, rubbing my back in soothing circles. 'But more importantly, people have seriously seen you naked?' Her innocent wide blue eyes stare back at me hoping for a different answer.

I gulp down the bile rising in my throat. I look around the cafe wondering who here has seen it. Seen my tits. My vagina. God, it's mortifying.

7

'I still can't believe it. How has my life become such a mess in twenty-four hours?' I throw my head down on the table dramatically, hoping someone will take pity and buy me a doughnut.

'Don't worry,' Brooke soothes, rubbing my shoulders. 'The good news is you have a great body.' I sit up to glare at her. She smiles cheekily. 'Plus, I told you, I've got Nicholas on it. If he can't take it down no-one can.'

Nicholas works in IT and is apparently a part time badass hacker.

'I don't even want to consider him not being able to.' The idea that it could be online forever has me shivering in fear. 'Wait, does that mean he's seen it?'

She rolls her eyes. 'Of course he's seen it. Most people have.'

I close my eyes and concentrate on breathing deeply. Nicholas has seen me naked. Everyone has seen me naked.

'So, what are you going to do about a new roommate?' Evelyn asks, always trying to look at stuff she can fix.

Probably best to stick to one crisis at a time.

'I'll have to find a new one. But I need one immediately. I can't afford to pay this month's rent on my own and that means I'll be evicted and get bad credit. Ugh, it's such a mess! All because Slut Barbie decided to choose bros over her ho.' I jokingly break down, throwing my head on the table. 'I was her ho, goddamnit!'

'You were whose ho?'

I look up to see Tom 'Manwhore' Maddens standing above me, his eyes dancing with amusement. God, just what I need, this tool. I didn't even know he was down from Peterborough.

I roll my eyes. 'I'm no one's ho.'

Dear God, don't let Tom have seen the picture. I'll have to kill myself. There'll be no other option. None.

Tom, and Erica's boyfriend Jack, sit down at the table. Tom leans forward and steals my hash brown, eating it like an apple.

'Hey!' I bark, trying and failing to snatch it back.

'Sorry,' he shrugs. 'I would have stolen some bacon but there isn't any.'

'She's a veggie remember?' Evelyn says with an eye roll.

God I *really* hope he hasn't seen the pictures. The idea of Tom seeing me naked makes me feel ill. I'm half waiting for a meat joke to fly my way.

'How did it go?' Erica asks Jack, her forehead furrowed with worry.

He sighs, and it's only then I notice the slight purplish bags under his eyes. 'Not so good.'

'What's going on?' I ask, looking between the two of them.

Jack sighs again as if the weight of the world is on his shoulders. 'I spoke to Amber about her attitude towards Erica. She's still saying you can't see Esme and that I can't bring her down here.'

God, I forgot that his bitch ex was doing that. Esme is Jack's four-year-old daughter from a previous relationship. She told Erica in no uncertain terms that she was a phase and Jack would soon be moving home to Peterborough.

Erica puts her head in her hands. 'I'm so sorry.'

'Why the hell are you sorry?' Evelyn asks her, clearly outraged. 'She's the one being an unreasonable cow.'

'That doesn't stop me feeling shit that he can't bring his daughter here.'

Bless Erica. I know she feels terrible regardless.

He stands behind her, massaging her shoulders. 'I'm more upset that my daughter can't spend time with the woman I love.'

'Awww!' we all chorus, half of us at how sweet they are, half of us at how gross they are.

I can't help but find them sickening. Partly because that's what I want. My other half. My one person to depend on no matter what. Sometimes I wonder if I'll ever find them. This whole naked thing is going to make me fussier.

'Anyway,' Tom says, clapping his hands as if to try to pull us all out of our depression. 'We have some good news for you girls.'

That's a way to get all our attention. Even Erica looks baffled, her eyes bouncing from Tom to Jack.

'Guess who's moving to Brighton?' he asks with a grin. He beams, pointing two fingers down at himself. 'This guy!'

He *has* to be kidding. That's the last thing I need. Jack's dickhead friend hanging around annoying me. Just when I thought this week couldn't get any worse.

'No way!' Molly squeals jumping up to give him a hug like the excitable bunny she is.

'So, the job interview went well, then?' Erica says, punching him on his shoulder. 'When do you start?'

He smiles back at her like a proud little boy. 'Next Monday, but it's only a temporary contract for the first few months. Apparently I've got to prove myself before they'll sign me up properly. So... I was hoping I can stay at yours until I find a place?'

Erica's eyes widen, staring intently at me. 'Well, this is perfect! Alice needs a new roommate and you're looking for somewhere.'

I look back at her as if she's stupid. Does she honestly think I'd live with this Neanderthal?

'Err, I don't think so,' I snort, unable to hide my disgust at the idea.

Tom's face falls, his piercing green eyes narrowing on me. 'Don't pretend you wouldn't love to live with me and play wife, Ice Queen.'

I fake a physical shudder. 'I would rather live with *anyone* than you.'

'But you were just saying how desperate you were,' Molly says, with a befuddled look on her face. I hate when she acts all dumb and innocent. We all know she's smart as hell and just plays on that silly blonde thing.

'Desperate for me, are you, baby?' Tom taunts, fluttering his eyelashes.

'Ugh, just shut up. You're not living with me. I'd rather get evicted.'

He writes down his number on the bill and hands it over. 'Whatever you say, Ice Queen. Call me when you come to your senses.'

'I'll let you know when hell freezes over.'

Tom

Nicholas snorts. 'There's no way Alice is going to let you live with her.'

I smirk. 'Mate, not only is she going to beg to live with me, but I'll be banging her before I move out.'

'Banging her?' Jack laughs. 'Fuck, you're delusional.'

I scoff confidently. 'Not only that, but I'll bag her too. Get her to fall for me.'

Nicholas creases over laughing. 'Don't make me die! She'd never fall for you. You're polar opposites.'

'She'll be in my bed, begging for my cock.'

They erupt laughing. 'Mate,' Jack chuckles, 'you've got

more chance of bagging a racoon than you have with Alice.'

'Wanna bet?' I ask, acting far cockier than I feel.

'I'd defo put a wager on that,' Nicholas nods, 'but I don't want you to lose your money.'

'I was just thinking the same about you,' I retort, too proud to back down.

'Fine,' Nic says, folding his arms in front of him. 'Let's call it fifty quid.'

I scoff. 'Make it a hundred.' Right now, I haven't got fifty pence to my name, but he doesn't have to know that.

'Done,' he says shaking my hand. Jack just rolls his eyes. 'Easiest money I ever made.'

'Prepare to eat your words.'

Operation 'Bagging Alice' is in progress.

Chapter 3

Alice

So, when I said I'd rather live with anyone, I was banking on actually finding someone. *Anyone.* But for a banging area like Cavendish Place in Brighton, and a gorgeous Georgian flat just off the beach, I can't find any fucker that wants to live with me.

Well, I say that. Apart from some sick bastards that have contacted me, clearly having seen me naked. The few normal people that do want to move in, want to do it in a few months. Need time to 'sort themselves out'. Bloody pussies.

So, I have two very limited options. Either I can't pay the rent and see how quickly they'll evict me. I mean, squatters have rights, don't they? Or the other, more painful option, is to let Tom 'Manwhore' Maddens move into my little piece of paradise. I can't even consider the third option: moving back home. I shudder at the idea.

Oh God. I'm going to have to do it. Swallow my pride and call him. Ask him to... gulp... live with me. God, it's such an awful idea, maybe I will have to think about moving back home. But that is even worse than living with that dickhead. My parents and I don't get on. They want me to be something I'm not.

I flatten up the bill with his number on and dial it into my mobile. It rings four times. Please let it go to voicemail. That'll be so much less humiliating.

'Yep,' he answers. What kind of person answers the phone like that? Yep?

'Hi. It's Alice.' I swallow, attempting to relieve my dry mouth. I'm as nervous as when I first spoke to a boy on the phone. I was fifteen then, and as I wait for him to answer it's as if no time has passed at all.

There's silence. 'Sorry. Alice...?'

He cannot be serious right now. 'Alice Watts, dickhead.' I spit through gritted teeth. 'You know it's me.'

'Oh, hi, Ice Queen,' he says, far too happily for my liking. I can just imagine his stupid face smirking and thinking how funny he is. 'How are you?'

God, I can't believe I have to back down to this idiot. Ask him to live with me. To take up residence in this funky flat I've managed to make my own. I look around at the turquoise walls and eclectic furniture I've bought over the years. He's not going to appreciate this. But then if he doesn't move in I'll lose it all anyway.

'Yeah, well...' I clear my throat and square my shoulders to fake confidence, even though he can't see me. 'I'm just calling to say if you want to move in here you can. But I have some conditions.'

'Oh r-e-a-l-l-y,' he answers smugly stringing out the word. 'And what makes you think I'm still interested?'

I clench my fists. The cocky bastard wants me to beg. Not going to happen.

'You're still sleeping on Erica and Brooke's sofa. I'm pretty sure you're still interested.'

I bloody hope he is. What if he's found somewhere by now?

'Fine,' he sighs. Oh, thank God. 'What are these *conditions*?' I can almost imagine him doing air quotes.

'Okay, number one. No bringing women back here.'

He makes a sound like he's just hit a buzzer. 'No way. Even my parents let me bring girls back.'

'Stop calling them girls. It makes you sound like you're bringing back schoolgirls. They're women.'

'Fine. Call them whatever you want, but if I'm paying half the rent I want my proper rights.'

I roll my eyes. 'What about if I agree not to bring back any guys too?'

He snorts a laugh. 'Yeah, like you'd be bringing guys back.'

'Sorry?' I challenge, clenching my hand around the phone. 'Are you trying to say that I can't pull?' Does he think I'm butt ugly or something?

'No, not that you can't, just that you don't. How long have I known you now, and I've never seen you hook up for a one-nighter?'

Calm down, Alice. He's just saying you're not a slag. That's a good thing. Well, maybe I *should* become a slapper. Look what happens when I try to stick to relationships.

'That doesn't mean I don't.'

He scoffs. 'Okay.'

God, this man is infuriating. 'Whatever, Tom. Take it or leave it. No whores back here or no room for you.'

I hold my breath, awaiting his answer. I hate to admit it, but I really need him. Nothing but silence greets me. Shit, he's going to say no. I'm screwed.

'Fine. But I move in tomorrow.'

Sunday 14th October

Alice

'Honey, I'm home!' Tom calls as he walks in carrying a huge box the next day. He's wearing jeans, and a navy t-shirt that's too tight for him. His stupid biceps are bulging out of it.

I jump up from the sofa. 'How did you even get in?' He hasn't got a key yet.

'Sorry,' Erica says from behind him, carrying a smaller box, 'I gave him my spare key.'

I run to her and shake her shoulders. 'Erica, are you sure you won't move in here with me, and we can leave the boys to live together?'

She raises her eyebrows. 'What, with Brooke? You know Nicholas has been jealous enough with Tom staying with us, right?'

Nicholas really needs to work on his jealousy issues, but Brooke seems to love the attention. It doesn't help that they used to hook up before she got together with Nicholas.

'Ugh. I can't believe I have to live with a boy.' I wail jokingly.

'Hey!' Tom protests. 'What was it you said on the phone? I'm a *man*, not a boy.'

Using my own words against me. How infuriating.

'Whatever.' I look down at the two boxes. 'So, is this all your stuff?' At least he packs light.

He laughs. 'Yeah, right.'

Jack walks in pushing a clothes rail full of suits. 'Hey, Alice. Which is his bedroom?'

'Jesus, you're more of a tart than I thought.'

'Yeah, yeah,' he dismisses with an eye roll. 'Just shut up and put an apple pie in the oven, woman.' He throws his butt down onto my emerald-green, crushed-velvet sofa, his hands behind his head. 'Time to make me feel at home.'

I take a deep breath and try to focus on not growling at him. I don't want to give him the rise he so obviously wants.

I pull Erica over to one side. 'Does Tom know about the pictures?' I whisper. That could be another reason he's so eager to move in with me. Thinks he's going to find me naked in the living room shaving my legs.

She shakes her head. 'No. Only Jack knows; apart from Nicholas, who's still trying to get the main site shut down. Apparently, the encryption is a nightmare. But I made them promise not to mention it to anyone else. Especially Tom.'

'Oh, thank God.'

If he knew about that, he'd only lord it over me. I could do without it.

Eight boxes, and three packages from IKEA later, and he's all moved in.

'How is it possible you have so much crap?' I ask, looking around at all the boxes.

'What can I say?' he shrugs. 'I like to take care of my appearance.' His eyes rake over my jeans and black tank top. 'You should try it some time.'

I roll my eyes. 'Whatever, Manwhore.'

'Anyway, we should get off,' Jack says looking at his watch. 'Alice, thanks for taking him off our hands.'

'Keep that sofa open. We may kill each other.'

The minute the front door closes behind them, the awkwardness creeps over me. We stare at each other. I can't believe I'm living with him.

'So...' he starts, 'you want to help me put my bed together?'

I raise my eyebrows at him. 'Is that what you say to all the girls?'

'Ha ha. We live together now. I don't shit where I eat, so that means no fucking for us two.'

I'm actually appalled that he thinks he needs to clarify this to me. I wouldn't touch him with a bargepole.

'How will I cope?' I deadpan.

'Now, I know right now all you want to do is cry into your pillow but come on. You can take your mind off it by helping me build my bed.'

I sigh, folding my arms over my chest. 'God, if it'll shut you up and get you into your bedroom, then fine.'

I follow him in and sit cross-legged on the floor while I read the instructions.

'This seems simple enough.'

Famous last words. It's a fucking nightmare. No wonder they sell their stuff so cheap, it's because you end up setting it on fire in frustration and buying another set.

'Where's the squiggly thing?'

'Ugh.' I throw myself down onto the floor. 'I don't know what a fucking squiggly thing is. I'm so over this!'

He sighs heavily, his normally line-free forehead deeply furrowed. 'Me too. I'm gonna have to sleep in your bed.'

That has me looking up at him. 'I don't bloody think so!' I shriek. 'Jesus, one night here and you're trying it on.'

He smirks. 'Don't flatter yourself, Ice Queen.'

'I hear the sofa is very comfortable,' I counter with a smug smile.

He lets out a heavy sigh. 'How can one piece of furniture cause so much stress?' He stands up and kicks the bed frame.

I stand up too and give it a kick. It feels good. I shove at it and kick it again. He joins in, and before we know it we're beating the shit out of the bed, screaming in rage.

We stop, out of breath and on the floor. His chest heaves, straining his muscles against his navy t-shirt. He catches me looking, I know he does, but I look away quickly and for once he's kind enough not to mention it.

'I'll get you some blankets for the sofa.'

Tom

I look at my watch. It's one am and I can't sleep on this shitty sofa. She must have found this in a skip as no person would willingly spend money on it, surely? It's one of those poncy arty sofa's that's all about the look and nothing about the comfort.

I stare up at the framed artwork on the wall: some vintage styled pin-up girl in the middle of an ace of hearts playing card. It's pretty cool. The whole flat is really. Well, it's totally Alice. An eclectic mix of mismatching furniture that somehow works alongside these pin-up pictures, plants, and hardwood floors.

I start my new job tomorrow, and I really don't want to be sleep deprived. I'd just pull out my new mattress and sleep on that, but with the half-built bed frame there's no room for it to go on the floor. She must have stolen the bigger room.

I could just sneak into bed with her. I shake my head. No, I can't do that. She'd kill me. There's no way she'd allow it. Plus, I don't want to scare her too much on my first night. But... what if she's already asleep? I mean, she should be at this time. Maybe I should just go and take a peep. See if she's passed out already.

I creep along the floorboards into the wide hallway that she's lined head-to-toe with books, and tentatively take hold of her door knob. It squeaks ever so slightly as I turn it. I wince, frozen in place, waiting to hear her shout out for me to fuck off. She doesn't, so I push it slowly open.

I feel a thrill of excitement as I realise this is the first time I'll see her room. A sliver of light from the hallway exposes its warm red walls, a few shades lighter than her hair. It's not how I imagined it to be. I'm not sure what I was expecting. Maybe something more like the sitting room.

Her black bedspread is covered in flower patterns and there are big fluffy pillows thrown on the floor. Her furniture is white and relatively plain, but on every wall are photos. Photos of her and the girls, photos of landscapes, photos of celebrities. So many of them. I wonder if she took some of those?

She's under the covers, lying face down on her stomach. One of her slim pale legs is poking out. She's wearing little shorts which have ridden up, so I can make out the curve of her arse cheek. I've always thought of her as skinny and almost boyish, but that's a good little arse. Her skin is so milky-white I'm kind of surprised she doesn't glow in the dark.

I creep over to the empty side of the bed, glad she hasn't starfished across the whole mattress. I look down at her, her mass of red hair shielding her face. It's grown since we all met at Luna Island.

She suddenly stirs, a soft moan filling the silent room. I freeze. Shit, what a way to be found. Watching her sleep. She'd kick me out and get a restraining order for sure. She rests her head back onto the pillow, this time half of her face is visible.

Even without make-up, she looks pretty much the same. The same flawless pale skin, thin lips with the most perfect cupid's bow, and long lashes. Although I'm shocked to see they're fair. Is she naturally blonde?

I pull the duvet back carefully and let myself into the bed, careful not to touch her. Ooh, it's memory foam. God, it's warm and cosy. I roll onto my side and watch her while I let sleep take a hold of me. She might act fierce, but up close like this, she's just another beautiful girl.

Chapter 4

Alice

I wake up naturally, like I do most mornings. It's typical that I don't have a regular job where I need to be at a desk at nine for and yet I still wake up before eight am. I push my arms over my head and indulge in a glorious stretch, moaning from the release of my tight muscles. My hand meets something hairy. Oh my god, is a mouse in my bed? Or worse, a hairy spider? Aren't the only hairy one's tarantulas that bite you and leave you paralysed?

'Aaarrrgh!' I scream, sitting up in bed and shaking my hand in the air.

I look over to where I'm expecting to see something causing me to run out of the front door and post a petrol bomb through the letterbox.

Instead, I find a sleeping, topless Tom. What the hell is he doing in my bed? I don't know if I'm relieved or more afraid.

He stirs, obviously from my ghoulish scream, eventually opening his eyes. I glare down at him with a hatred I feel deep in my soul.

'Tom. What the fuck are you doing in my bed?' I screech, using the duvet to cover me up as best as possible. Thank God, I didn't sleep naked.

He looks around, his creased eyes slowly adjusting to the light, as if trying to remember where he is. 'Oh yeah. Oops.'

He is unbelievable. 'Oops! This wasn't a fucking accident. You snuck in here in the middle of the night and got into my bed! People have been arrested for less.'

He stretches out, exposing dark-blonde hair under his armpits. 'Oh, chill out. I needed a good night's sleep before I start work today. Now, how about I make it up to you by making some bacon and pancakes?'

'I'm a vegi-fucking-tarian,' I growl, my muscles twitching with rage. 'You bloody know this, you imbecile.'

'Oh yeah.' He chuckles to himself. 'I keep forgetting bacon is meat.'

I frown. Can someone really be that dense?

'I take it you have pancake mix though, right?' He smiles hopefully. How can he be so carefree when he's totally overstepped a boundary line?

'I don't bloody know. Isn't it just some flour and eggs?'

He frowns. 'Don't worry, I'll Google it, roomie.'

He climbs out of the bed in only his tight black boxer shorts, stretching so high he pushes the ceiling. Damn it, he really needs to put a shirt on. He's got muscles on top of muscles. It's been a while since I've seen a man look that good undressed, and the closeness of having him in my bedroom is doing strange things to me. Shit. If this is how unsettled I feel after day one, how am I going to feel after a month?

It's only a month, Alice. I'll keep looking for someone, maybe one of the people that couldn't move in straightaway. Just ride this month out and then I'll be fine and rid of Tom 'Manwhore' Maddens for good.

By the time I made it out to the kitchen, the place was destroyed. I'm not even being dramatic. Pancake sludge was everywhere. What I thought was flour covered every surface and much of the floor. He proudly presented me with two pancakes that were burned around the edges.

'As a sorry gift,' he'd said.

Well maybe it would have worked if they were edible. As soon as I put the lumpy pancake into my mouth, I knew I had to spit it out. It tasted rank. Turns out when he found I had no flour, he'd thought baking powder could be a fine alternative. You know, being that they're both white. Fucking idiot.

Then he rushed off to work claiming he couldn't be late on his first day, leaving me to clean it all up. To say I'm fuming is an understatement.

I need to get his bed built somehow today. I can't have him thinking he can sleep in my bed again. Fucking pervert. I wouldn't put it past him to have groped a boob while he had the chance. I should call the police on the man.

So I call Brooke and together we work it out, putting it together before I have to run off to photograph a newborn. Thankfully there's a mum who liked my work so much she doesn't care I'm now an unofficial FHM model now.

Tom best be bloody grateful.

Evelyn and Brooke attach me to a WhatsApp group titled *'Fight for Alice'*. Jesus, with those two I dread to think what it could be. Someone starts typing so I wait patiently.

Brooke: Me and Evelyn have been talking

Evelyn: And we think we need to have a word with the police about those photos.

Brooke: Yeah, I keep getting them emailed to me. And no offence, babe, but there's only so many times I can look at your tits. Plus, Nic says he's having trouble getting the site shut down. Whenever he thinks he's cracked it, it ends up being back up within the hour.

Evelyn: He shouldn't be able to get away with this!

Me: Okay, I'm in. What's the plan?

Tom

The first day at my new job was a bitch. What they failed to tell me in the interview is that I have a female boss. Now, before you start shouting about feminism and equality in the work place, I'm not against women being above me. Or under me for that matter. But this woman doesn't like me. I could tell it the moment she laid eyes on me.

Bernice Shuttlecock. That's right. Her surname is shuttlecock. And she insists on everyone calling her Mrs Shuttlecock. Every time I say it I can't help but get a stupid grin on my face and have to literally bite my tongue to stop from laughing. Maybe that's why she doesn't like me?

Anyway, she's in her early fifties, wears fishnet stockings far too inappropriate for her age, and she's strict. She expected me to know all their product lines off by heart on the first day and kept trying to trip me up. Then she made it even weirder by checking me out when I dropped my notebook. Freaky.

So, I've brought home the catalogue and I intend to study the hell out of it. I hate being made to look stupid.

Then I remember I'm going to have to face Alice and her wrath when I get in. I hesitate at the door, wondering if I should go for a quick pint first. No. I need a clear head to learn. I take a deep breath, broaden my shoulders and walk in.

A gorgeous smell assaults my nostrils. Something is cooking, and it smells awesome. It's the first time I've actually missed my mum since being here. She likes to feed her little prince. My stomach rumbles. God, I'd love nothing more than a homemade dinner by Mum right now.

'Honey, I'm home!' I shout as I walk down the corridor and into the open plan kitchen/living room.

She's dressed in grey sweatpants with a black tank top on, no bra. Shit, they may be small tits, but they're pert as fuck, her nipples straining against the fabric. *Do not get a boner. Do NOT get a boner.*

'Hey,' she says absentmindedly as she bends over the worktop, pen in her mouth, trying to figure out a crossword. God, how I'd love to bend her over.

'I didn't realise people under sixty did those.'

Her eyes flare. God, I love pissing her off. It excites something deep inside me.

'*Some* of us like to exercise our brains, not just our muscles. You should try it some time.'

I snort and hold up the catalogue. 'Yeah, well I've got to learn the product codes for this entire thing. If that's not working your brain, I don't know what is.'

She grimaces. 'How was your first day?'

'Rough.' I sigh. 'My boss hates me.'

This news seems to make her happy, a smug smile gracing her perfect lips. 'You sound surprised. Not everyone falls in love with you the minute they meet you, you know?'

I snort a laugh. 'Tell that to the female population of Peterborough.'

She rolls her eyes. 'Anyway, you're gonna be happy with me.'

'Really?' I enquire, a bit too eager. I have to lighten the mood. I plaster a grin on. 'You've decided I can pay my half of the rent with sexual favours?' She grimaces in disgust. I've never seen someone look so disgusted. 'It's a good plan. You need to work off some of this tenseness.' I poke her in her side.

She flinches overdramatically. 'Don't touch me, Tom.'

Wait a sec. Is she ticklish?

'Is someone scared of the tickle monster?' I joke, flexing my fingers threateningly in the air.

Her sea-green eyes blaze. 'I mean it, Tom, fuck off. I'm not in the mood. I had to clean up your shit show of a pancake mess this morning. Which brings me to another point.'

I grab the stool and sit down, ready for a lecture. 'Okay, shoot.'

'Don't tempt me,' she mutters under her breath. 'Okay, first of all, me and Brooke have fixed your bed.' My mouth drops open in disbelief. Girls doing DIY. That sounds like some awesome porn. 'So, no more sneaking into my bedroom at night. The next time you do, I'll be calling the police.'

I scoff a laugh and put my hands up in protest. 'Okay, cuddle bunny. Understood. But don't pretend you didn't enjoy the spooning.'

She grits her teeth and chooses to ignore that one.

'Second, I'm guessing if that's how you attempt to cook pancakes, you have no experience with cooking?'

I hold my palms up. 'Guilty!' She rolls her eyes. 'Hey, I can't help it that I have a mum who loves me and wants to make sure her strapping son eats well.'

'Your mother has done you no favours. She's made you useless.' That hurts more than it should. 'So, I'll be doing the cooking around here. I don't want you to do anything harder than toast some bread. Am I understood?'

'Yes, Miss,' I joke giving her a soldier salute. God, this is amazing. First, she's fixed my bed, now she's going to cook for me. I picked the right roomie for sure.

'But you'll be doing the washing up, and the cleaning of the kitchen.'

Ugh, just when I thought it was going well.

'If you don't know how to wash pans I'll stand over you and instruct,' she adds sarcastically.

'Will you have a whip?' I joke, giving her my best sexy smoulder.

Another glare. She's too easy to wind up.

I open the catalogue and start trying to memorise everything. I now work for a consumer electronics company so it's a load of TV's, DVD players, and set top boxes. Possibly the most boring job in the world, but the pay is good.

Before I register how much time has passed, she's putting a dinner in front of me and sitting down on the other side of the kitchen table.

I look down at my curry. God, it looks and smells amazing.

'Thanks!' I take my fork and dig in. It's delicious, but something isn't right. 'This chicken tastes different. What have you done to it?'

Oh God. I knew she was being too nice. She's poisoned me, hasn't she? I'm going to fall to the floor clutching at my throat as foam falls from my mouth. Until I take my last breath, as Alice looks over me with a sick, satisfied smile.

She smirks. 'That's because it's Quorn, bonehead.'

I frown. 'Quorn. What the fuck is Quorn?'

She sighs, as if exhausted by me. 'A meat alternative. I'm a vegetarian, remember?'

Ugh, she's feeding me fake meat. That is so evil.

'Wait, wait, wait. So because you're a vegetarian, that means I'm no longer allowed to eat the good stuff?'

She shrugs. 'You can eat meat; it's just that all my meals won't have any. But feel free to put steak cutlets in with your cereal.'

I huff. 'Look, I'm not saying this isn't delicious, but I'm a growing lad. I need protein.'

She rolls her eyes. 'Jesus, Tom. Open a book once in a while. Quorn is full of protein as are the chickpeas and beans.'

'So, you're saying my muscles aren't going to waste away?' I still don't believe her.

She scoffs. 'Don't worry, muscle man, they're safe.'

I look back down at the catalogue, dreading diving back in after washing up.

'How are you getting on?' she asks nodding towards it.

'Shit. It's hard enough remembering all of the products, but they want us to learn the product codes too, and it might as well be fucking Chinese to me.'

She takes the catalogue from me and studies it a bit, her forehead wrinkling in concentration. It's kind of adorable. Shit, maybe she has poisoned me. Since when do I find birds adorable?

'Okay, I think I've got it.'

'Got what?' I ask, swallowing down my last delicious mouthful. The girl can cook, I'll give her that.

'Got the way they code stuff. Like here.' She points to a

TV. 'GTVR2DVSTB015. So, G stands for the brand, then TV means TV, duh. R2 is the model number. DV means built in DVD player. STB means it has set top box functionality. And then 015 is the year it was made.'

I look back at her in amazement. 'You worked that all out in two minutes? I've been staring at those codes all day.'

She shrugs. 'You just have to think about what the codes mean and it's easy enough. Like here, take a guess what an Alva branded TV with set top box functionality would be?'

'Okay, it's Alva so A... TV... STB?' I guess, feeling stupid.

'Yes!' she says punching the air far too excitedly. 'And it's 016 because that's the year it was made.'

This actually makes some fucking sense.

After showing me how to wash up to her standards (fussy bitch) she spends all night quizzing me, and by midnight she only needs to point to a product picture and I'm shouting out the code like a trained monkey.

'Thanks, Alice. Who knew you'd be helpful with shit like this.'

'Not just a pretty face,' she smiles, flicking her hair over her shoulder. It's just about flickable length.

'Not even that,' I wink, bursting out laughing.

She curls her lip up in anger, but her eyes say something else. Did I hurt her feelings? I was only taking the piss, having a bit of banter.

'Just when I think you might be an okay human being.' She jumps up, goes to her room and slams the door. Whoops.

Chapter 5

Alice

Just when I actually start to think he might be a half-decent human being, he goes and calls me ugly. How fucking dare he? Every insecurity I've ever had rears its ugly head, pushing past thoughts to the surface.

I got picked on at school for a myriad of things. My deathly pale complexion meant I was called dead or a vampire daily. I wore glasses and had train-track braces. I tried my best to blend in as much as I could. I laugh when I think about it now.

That low confidence is what found me with an ungrateful boyfriend that constantly belittled me. We were living together by the time I was seventeen and it took me a long time to wake the fuck up and realise what a prize tool he was.

It helped when I found the text messages on his phone. Laughing with his bit on the side about how little of an idea I had. Mocking me. That's probably what hurt the most. The person that was supposed to love me most in the world taking the piss out of me.

From that day, I vowed to never attempt to blend in

again. After all, it had got me nowhere. I moved out and got residence in halls at Brighton university. A fresh start where I could re-invent myself. I scoured Pinterest for hours looking for a new image. In the end it took a walk through Brighton for me to decide how I wanted to look.

I saw a beautiful woman with the same pale skin as me. She had bright red hair, tattoos, piercings, and wore a navy-blue polka-dot dress with the most stunning red shoes. She was going into a Rockabilly festival.

I went home and googled Rockabilly. These people seemed to favour the fifties and enjoy all things vintage. I'd always been obsessed with that time. Apparently, I watched *Grease* so many times when I was younger, my mum banned me from eating those candy cigarettes and saying, *'Tell me about it, stud.'* She's always been a killjoy.

So, I bought a glorious red hair colour from *Superdrug* and dyed my dark-blonde hair. I set out to change everything about myself. Over the next six months I got piercings, tattoos, and shopped to my heart's content. Before buying something, I wouldn't ask myself *'what will people think?'*, instead I'd ask myself *'do I love it?'*

And I've never been happier. But when that dickwad just called me ugly it pulled that awkward, unsure of herself Alice, to the forefront. And for that I hate him.

We can't all be born with God-like features. Some of us have to work at it.

I hear the front door slam. Thank God. For a few hours I can pretend I live on my own again.

The door knocks a few minutes later. Oh God, the idiot's obviously forgotten his keys. I'll have to get him a necklace with a key on it. I stomp towards the door, ready to tear him a new one. Instead I find Brooke and Evelyn there.

'Don't shoot!' Brooke says, her eyes twinkling with comedy. 'What's got you looking so pissed?'

'Huh, how long have you got?'

'Whatever,' Evelyn says, passing me as she texts. No doubt her boyfriend Omar from Luna Island. I still find it shocking that they've managed all these months with being in different countries, but hey, it works for them. 'We need to make a plan. Tomorrow we report your revenge porn.'

Tom

God, I hate an atmosphere. I already feel like a massive bellend for upsetting Alice, but with her storming off to her room it's not like I could fix it. So that's how I found myself grabbing my coat and walking to the local pub, where I'm currently chatting up some easy brunette who's been giving me so many green lights it's verging on embarrassing.

She leans over, giving me a view of her ample cleavage. 'How about we get out of here?'

I was waiting for her to offer. I don't think it would go down too well if I brought her back to the flat. Not with my no girls rule. Or no women rule as Alice likes to call it. God, that broad gets under my skin. I'm supposed to be charming her into bed to win my bet with Nicholas, but the woman is so infuriating I don't think I'll be able to.

Within minutes we're jumping in a taxi and making it back to her flat. I can't help but notice that ours is far nicer, even with Alice's crazy taste. I push her against her bedroom wall and start kissing her neck. She's far more olive-skinned than Alice. Alice is so pale she's like a porcelain doll. Wait, why the fuck am I thinking about Alice right now?

Get your head in the game, Tom.

I grab one of her tits and squeeze while I grind my dick up against her. This chick's tits are massive. I don't even know why I was thinking of Alice. She's got itty bitty titties. Barely a handful I reckon. But then they are pert... and her nipples always seem to be erect. Poking out from every single top she wears, trying to provoke me.

'Ooooh!' she coos, before sticking her tongue down my throat. Fuck, why aren't I into this? I need to just fucking get on with it.

I throw her onto her bed and tear at her top. She throws it off over her head and has her skirt at her ankles before you can say *that was unnervingly easy for her.* It's clear she's no virgin, but then again neither am I.

I undo my jeans, letting them fall to my ankles. I take out a condom, carefully put it on and then hover over her.

'Oh Gooooooooood!' she coos like a porn star. 'Do me! Do me now!'

Ugh.

I pick her up and turn her around so she's on all fours. I don't want to be looking at her if she's going to be making those ridiculous noises. I thrust into her, not caring enough to warm her up first. Low and behold she's as wet as an otter's pocket. Dirty bitch.

I fuck out all of my frustration; thrust after thrust making me more relaxed. Fucking Alice annoying the hell out of me. Who the hell does she think she is?

The light catches the woman's hair and for a second it has a tinge of redness to it. I imagine it's Alice I'm fucking some sense into, and suddenly my mojo is back. I slap her arse and bite her shoulder.

'Yeah, baby,' she screams. 'I'm going to come!'

God, why does she insist on talking? She's totally ruining my vibe.

'I'm coming! I'm coooooooooooooming!'

And that's my erection gone. For the first time in my life, I fake my own orgasm, remove the condom before she notices, and get the hell out of there.

Chapter 6

Tuesday 16th October

Alice

Tom snuck back some time last night and out again early this morning before I woke up. I only know he came back at all because his protein shake container was in the sink. The stinky fucking thing. He couldn't even be bothered to rinse it out. Lazy fucker. His mother has ruined him.

Anyway, I have more important things to worry about. Like how us girls find ourselves waiting in the police station the next morning, expecting a PC Graeme Edwards to come talk to us.

'Hi,' a giant of a guy says, suddenly in front of me. He towers over us. Thank God, he's one of the good guys, otherwise I'd fear the dude. He must be at least six-foot-three and sports a goatee. 'I'm PC Edwards. Come with me, ladies.'

We're led into a room that smells of new paint, with a wooden table and blue plastic chairs. It's not like how I imagined, but then I do watch a lot of US based cop shows. I kind of think I was expecting a dark room with a two-way window.

He gets out a notebook and pen. 'So, your friends told me on the phone that an ex-boyfriend has posted private naked photos of you. Is that correct?'

'Yes,' I nod, swallowing hard at the reminder. It's so embarrassing having to talk about it out loud. 'It's on a site called *Revenge Porn Utopia*. I can email you the link.'

He nods, writing stuff down. 'That would be helpful. And do you have any proof that your ex-boyfriend is the one behind this?'

'It's fucking obvious!' Brooke exclaims, throwing her hands up in the air.

'Way to keep it classy,' Evelyn snorts, rolling her eyes at Brooke. 'Sorry,' she apologises to the policeman, 'just ignore her.'

I chew my lip, trying to think if I have anything solid. 'I suppose I don't have any rock-hard evidence. Just my word that he was the only person I sent the picture to.'

He grimaces slightly. Shit, does that mean there's no hope? That the case has collapsed before it's even fully opened?

'Okay, can I have his name?'

'Yep, Ted Cundy.'

He looks up mid-writing and stares at me. 'And the fact his name was like Ted Bundy didn't ring any alarm bells?'

I look to the girls, not sure if he's joking.

'Sorry, just my sense of humour!' he snorts. 'Very unprofessional of me.'

Brooke bursts out laughing. 'I've been calling him Ted Cunty. I didn't think of the Bundy thing.'

Trust Brooke to say the word cunt to a police officer. I raise my eyes heavenwards.

'Do you think you'll be able to get it taken down?' I ask, ignoring her.

'We'll contact the site owners and tell them to remove

the photo due to it being involved in a police investigation, and we'll send an officer around there to arrest him. We'll seize any computer items and send them to our high-tech crime unit.'

'And they can prove if he posted it?' I ask eagerly.

'They can use the IP data to see if it was the computer that posted the photo. It can take a number of weeks though.'

'But if you can prove that, you've got him, right?'

'Well, then we'll be able to interview him. Depending on the amount of evidence we're able to obtain from high-tech crime we might then be able to send on to the Crown Prosecution Service. It'll be up to them to decide whether to charge him or not.'

God, it's all so confusing.

My stomach sinks. 'Shit, what if he claims someone else posted it on his laptop? Is there anything else you can do but tell him off?'

It feels like too big a deal for just a bloody slap on the wrist.

'I had it emailed to me,' Brooke interjects. 'Surely you can trace the IP address from that too? My boyfriend's been trying to take down the site, but it's always back up within an hour.'

'Ah, now that's something we can do,' he says more positively. 'If you could forward the email to me.' He passes both of us his card. 'And if anything else changes or progresses, feel free to contact me directly. Any time of the night.'

Evelyn is putting on her sexy eyes. She obviously thinks that's his way of chatting her up.

'Thank you.'

But I know as well as the girls, nothing will ever come of this. What a colossal waste of time.

Alice

He's late home tonight. I know he's avoiding me, but I'm trying desperately not to care. He's probably out shagging everything he can in Brighton. Good luck to the dickhead.

I must have nodded off on the sofa when I get woken by the front door slamming. Damn it, I wanted to be in bed by the time he got in. He saunters in, throwing his keys on the hallway table.

'Oh,' he says when he spots me on the sofa. 'I didn't think you'd still be up.'

I shrug. 'I fell asleep. So, I wasn't waiting up for you or anything,' I add quickly.

He winks. 'Course you weren't, sweetheart.'

I roll my eyes. He's so bloody full of himself. How can one person be so bloody self-assured?

I get up to walk past him towards my bedroom but something moving across the floor catches my eye. I freeze as soon as I realise it's a giant, big arse spider. FUCK! My worst nightmare.

Maybe if I stay still it won't notice me and will go back to the depths of hell where it belongs.

Of course it doesn't though. It instead darts towards me, its eight spindly legs faster than Usain Bolt.

'Aargh! Aargh!' I scream, jumping up on the coffee table. 'Kill it!' I yell at Tom.

His eyes are twice the size of normal. 'What?' he asks, like a stupid bloody male.

'Kill it! KILL IT!' I screech, jumping up and down so hard I'm sure the table is going to cave in.

'Okay, calm your tits,' he shouts, a stupid smile at the edges of his mouth.

He starts walking towards it, but his stupid giant footsteps startle it. It starts running towards me again.

'Shit!' I scream, leaping into the air and jumping onto him. I scramble high up him, holding onto his neck, my legs clinging on like a koala bear's. 'Kill it!' I shriek, my voice so high it breaks. At this rate I'm going to have to burn the flat down.

'I can't see it,' he shouts, staggering backwards with my weight.

I scramble even higher, clambering with my hands around his face.

'Now I can't see anything!' he shouts, stumbling forward.

His shin hits the front of the coffee table making him fall forwards. We're going down. We slam onto the sofa like a sack of potatoes. I fly down next to him, my arm crushed by his big stupid body.

'Crap,' I say, out of breath, still wondering where that bastard spider is. It's as if I can feel it on me. Probably trying to get in my ear and lay hundreds of spider babies.

He stares back at me, his eyes incredulous. 'So, I take it you don't like spiders?'

'Shit,' I gasp. It's still alive. I jump onto the back of the sofa.

He jumps up and eventually stamps his foot down. 'There. Dead.'

I put my hand to my chest, feeling my erratic heartbeat returning to normal.

'Is it really dead? I want to see its body,' I demand. I don't trust that he isn't lying. Anything to get me to calm the fuck down.

He rolls his eye and lifts his shoe. There are the remnants of the squashed spider.

'Excellent,' I nod, swallowing down the fear.

He grins. 'I thought you were a vegetarian. Aren't you guys supposed to be friends with all animals?'

'Not spiders.' I shudder. 'They're different altogether.'

He smiles devilishly. 'Well, at least now I know your weakness.'

'I swear to God, Tom, if you ever threaten me with a spider I will fucking murder you in your sleep.'

He creases over laughing. 'You make me die, Alice!'

Well, I suppose that's one way to break the ice between us.

Chapter 7

Alice

'So,' Brooke presses over coffee at hers the next morning. 'How's it going living with hot stuff?' She wiggles her eyebrows suggestively.

I roll my eyes. 'It's a nightmare. Although I've found one good reason to keep him around.'

Her eyes nearly burst out of their sockets. 'No! Oh my god, Alice! Tell me everything.'

I stare back at her, dazed. What the hell is she going on about? Wait... does she think I mean I slept with him?

'Ew, no! Brooke, you're gross.' What the hell is she like?

She cackles, her eyes alight with mischief. 'It's not gross. It's only a matter of time between you both.'

How random is she being? Just because we're temporarily living together does not mean we're going to bone. That's like saying men and women can't be just friends. Tom and I aren't even that.

'You have met us both separately, right? You do know how much of a long shot that is?'

She wiggles her eyes. 'Not that long a shot, I'm telling

you,' she grins. 'And you'd be in for a treat. He could fuck you into next week.'

'Ewww!' I shriek. 'Too much information, Brooke.' The thought of them two having sex is too much.

She throws back her head in a hysterical laugh. 'Anyway, we need to talk business.'

She's called me here today saying she has an idea for a joint business venture. With her being a designer, I don't really understand what she could do for me. I already edit my own pictures.

It has me worried. I know I'm not earning good money at the moment with all my clients cancelling—no doubt because they've heard I'm some whore that poses naked—but I'm not sure about blending business and friendship. Besides, I've been thinking I need to go back to reaching my goal of being a fashion photographer. That's what I always wanted to be.

'So, you know how I found Erica reading that embarrassing romance book about a month ago?'

I smile at the memory. 'God, we ribbed her. What was it called again?'

'Barefoot Detective.'

We both collapse over again in hysterics.

'Anyway,' she continues, stirring sugar into her coffee, 'it got me thinking about book covers.'

'Riiight?' Where is she going with this?

'So, I joined a load of book groups on Facebook to do my research and custom-made covers can go for anything up to £600.'

'Shit.' That's crazy. Just for a book cover?

'Exactly. So... I'm thinking with your photography and my graphic design we could make ourselves a little side business doing this. What do you think?'

Wow. It's actually an idea that's not completely crazy. I feel bad for doubting her so easily.

'Well... I *was* going to say that we shouldn't involve ourselves in a business relationship,' I admit.

Her face drops. 'Oh.'

'But... for that sort of money I'd consider it.' Her face lights up again. 'How would we divide the money?'

'Sixty, forty. I'd handle all of the advertising and reaching out to clients and once you've photographed you just send me the files and I do the rest.'

It does sound good. And it's not like I'm booked back to back with clients.

'Okay,' I shrug. 'Why the hell not? If it means I get to pay the rent, it'll be worth it.'

'Great,' she beams. 'Now, we should probably do a few mock-up covers to show off our skills. I've already asked Nicholas, and he's refusing point blank.'

I giggle. I can't imagine him wanting to pose around like a pretty boy.

'But Jack is up for it as long as it's nothing too risqué.'

'Okay, great.' I already know he's mad photogenic.

'I was hoping that you'd also ask Tom.' She grimaces. Oh hell no.

'What? Why the hell do we need *him*?' He'd just love me begging him to take his shirt off.

'Oh, come on, Alice. You know as well as I do that it would be weird for me to ask him. He might get the idea I'm trying to chat him up or something.'

I roll my eyes. 'He knows you're with Nicholas now.' Not that I reckon it'd stop him. The guy has no standards. I wouldn't be surprised if he fucked his friend over.

'Yeah, and you know how crazy jealous he gets. I don't want to give him an excuse to think I'm still hung up on Tom.'

It's true. I've seen him sulk when Brooke flirted with a bartender. She just loves the attention.

'I still can't believe you ever slept with that Neanderthal.' *Who I now live with.*

She snorts. 'Don't diss it 'til you try it. He's great.'

I really can't imagine that. Surely with him just having one-night-stands, he'd be a selfish lover. Out for all his pleasure and not interested in yours.

'What, better than Nicholas?' I can't help but ask. I've always wondered.

'No! Of course not,' she snaps. 'With Nicholas it's completely different.' Her eyes become dreamy. 'It's so raw and passionate. He even...' she stops to blush. Brooke blushing. Jesus, what is he into?

'Brooke, I don't think I have *ever* seen you blush. What the hell did you do? Did he buy you a sex swing or something?'

She snorts a laugh. 'No, nothing like that. He...' More blushing. 'Well he told me he wants us to live together.'

I dribble out some coffee. 'Oh my god, that's amazing! Did you agree?'

'Yeah,' she nods, covering her face with her hair. 'God, it all feels so girly and cringe talking about it, but... God, I'm fucking nuts about him. In fact, I don't know how much longer I can cope with us living apart, so it makes sense.' Brooke gushing about a guy is still so strange to me and now she's so in love with Nicholas.

'Really? So, what's holding you back?'

She sighs, slumping her shoulders. 'He doesn't want to leave his dad after the heart attack. He's all better now, but he's worried he'll be lonely.'

'Oh,' I nod. I get why she doesn't understand that. Like me, she's not grown up close to her parents. We both got out as soon as we could. 'And you wouldn't move to Peter-borough?'

'Yuk!' she screeches dramatically, like I just told her to consider Iraq.

'It's really not that bad!' I snort. 'And it's so cheap you could probably buy.'

'You move there, then,' she retorts with raised eyebrows. 'Besides, now that I've found my dad I don't want to move far away from him.' She only recently re-united with him after growing up not knowing who he was. 'So…'

'So…?' I press. God, what has she done?

She cracks a devilish smile. 'I've put his dad on Tinder.'

'You've WHAT?' Only Brooke would be nuts enough to put a middle-aged man on Tinder when he has no intention of dating.

'Yep,' she nods. 'I made his profile last night. There's already been some matches.' She starts taking her phone out of her bag.

'You are fucking insane. He'll never go for it.'

She starts flicking through pictures. 'But what if he does? Some of these are alright looking. Problem solved.'

I get up and collect my bag from the back of the chair. 'Whatever, don't involve me. I don't want to be involved when it all blows up in your face.'

'It won't,' she says, sounding hurt. 'Just ask Tom about the photos, yeah?'

'Maybe,' I call after me before slamming the door shut.

Tom

Dad called me today to find out how I was doing. Find out if I'd fucked up yet more like. The thing that I haven't told the others is that my dad all but kicked me out. Told me he was sick of me treating the place like a hotel. Or did he use the word brothel? I've forgotten.

Not even a happy birthday call to my mate back home, Charlie, managed to cheer me up, and he was complaining about his nutty family. I normally piss myself over that shit.

I'm barely in the flat when Alice starts being nice to me. It's unnerving as hell. She clearly wants something.

'Why are you being so nice?' I ask as she serves me a cup of tea.

She looks hot as fuck today in black and white houndstooth cropped trousers, and a tight black t-shirt that's just short enough to see a glimpse of her stomach. Her hair is scooped up with one of those head scarfs she likes to wear wrapped around it.

'Can't I just be pleasant?' she shrugs with a wide grin, kicking off her red-and-white polka-dot heels and collapsing next to me on the sofa.

'Okay.'

She lets out a huge sigh. 'Ugh, I can't do it. Alright, there's something I need to ask you.'

I smirk. 'I knew it. Go on then.' She clearly wants a piece of Maddens.

She turns to face me. 'Right, well...' She squirms awkwardly, twiddling with a ring on her finger.

Wait a second. She *does* want to do a friends-with-benefits thing?

'I know what you're going to say,' I nod knowingly, a grin splitting my lips apart.

She frowns, her red lips falling open slightly. 'You do?'

'I do,' I nod, trying not to come across as too arrogant.

'You want to make a friends-with-benefits arrangement. That's fine, but we need some ground rules.'

She starts to smile. She's happy I've said it for her. Then she bursts out laughing.

'God, you're such a tool.'

'Huh?' Wait, she doesn't want my dick?

'I don't want to sleep with you, you twat.'

'You don't?' I'm genuinely confused. I was sure she secretly wanted me. What the hell else could she want to ask me?

She rolls her eyes. 'Of course I don't. Jesus, Tom, not everyone wants to shag you. It's actually quite sad that you think that's all your worth.'

What the hell does that mean?

'What I wanted to ask was if you'd mind posing semi-naked for a book cover?'

I stare back at her. Is this another joke? Is she setting me up just so she can ridicule me again?

'You want me to what now?' I blurt out, growing tired.

She starts explaining that her and Brooke are starting a new business venture and they want me to be the model. Of course they do, I'm hot.

'So, what exactly would I get out of this?' I ask with raised eyebrows, my tongue suggestively at the side of my mouth.

'Bragging rights?' she offers weakly. I raise my eyebrows. As if I'd do it for nothing. 'Okay,' she finally relents, 'we'll also pay you a hundred quid if we sell the photo.'

'That's more like it.' I could do with the extra cash. 'And my pictures aren't going to end up online for some haemorrhoid cream advert or something, right?'

I see it cross her mind. Evil cow.

She chuckles. 'No, don't worry. They'd be exclusively for book covers. Although now you mention that...'

Knew it. I love when she tries to tease me. 'And you'll be taking the pictures?'

She nods. 'I will.'

The thought of forcing her to look at my half naked body through a lens has a thrill going straight to my dick. She won't be able to resist me for long after that.

'Okay, I'm in. As long as you can control yourself.'

She rolls her eyes. 'Somehow I think I'll manage.'

It's so sweet how she thinks she can resist me. Only a matter of time before she's in my bed and I'm collecting my winnings from Nicholas.

Chapter 8

Thursday 18th October

Alice

Today I'm shooting Tom's pictures after he finishes work. I've been looking around all day for inspiration of where to shoot and I've decided on the beach. It's an easy all-rounder. He can take his top off, and look all muscly and pout, or whatever. He'll probably freeze half to death with it being particularly chilly today. Added bonus.

Jumping from foot to foot, I try to warm myself up as I wait for him. I wrap my coat around myself. I love this coat. I got it in a vintage market. It's bright red with a leopard print fur trim and so comfortable. Coats these days are so cheaply made; you can really tell the quality in stuff made years ago.

I'm just about to give up on him, having waited forty-five minutes past the time we agreed, when he finally sneaks up behind me.

'Hey, short stuff,' he says, all smiles like he hasn't just had me waiting for all of this time.

'Hey yourself, arsehole,' I snap, teeth gritted. 'Would it

have fucking killed you to send a text and say you were running late?'

He rolls his eyes. 'Chill out, Ice Queen. I was held up at work. My boss wanted to tell me what a good job I was doing.'

'Oooh, well, I'm *very* sorry that you were too busy getting praised at work to worry about little old me.'

'You really are little, aren't you?' he smirks, patting me on the head. I'm five foot two. Hardly a midget.

'You did not just pat me on the head, motherfucker!' I push him away from me with both of my hands. I could so easily wrap them around his neck and throttle him.

'Jesus, calm down, woman!' he says, his hands over his face in a defensive way. Like I'm actually gonna beat the crap out of him. Well... there's still time.

'You are the most insensitive, pompous prick I've ever met in my life.' I wail, hitting him on the chest. He barely flinches, damn muscly bastard.

He smirks and does a little bow. 'Why, thank you.'

'Aargh.' I scream in frustration, turning to pick up my camera bag, ready to bolt. 'This has been a complete waste of time.'

He stops me walking past him by grabbing my arm. Not painfully, but firmly enough to stop me. I look up into his piercing green eyes, my jaw set.

'I'm sorry,' he says quietly. I look into his eyes and see he is being genuine. Something extraordinarily rare from him.

My anger starts to dissipate slightly. I sigh, attempting to chill myself out a bit more. I hate how he brings out my inner nutcase.

'Fine. Do you still want to do this?'

'Yeah, course.' He throws his suit jacket on the floor,

pulls his tie out and over his head and then starts unbuttoning his shirt. I hate how it's hot.

'You're just gonna get changed here?' I roll my eyes. 'No shame,' I say under my breath, but loud enough for him to hear.

He takes his shirt off, showing off his muscular frame. How is he always so bronzed? I bet he goes on a sunbed, the tart. His nipples turn into erect little buds from the chill.

'Fuck, it's cold,' he complains.

He undoes his trousers, pulls them down and changes into the jeans we'd agreed on. He gets a few stares from passers-by, which he doesn't even seem to notice.

'Right, I'm thinking if we go down close to the shore and have you lying on your side.'

He grins. 'You've been wanting to get me in this position for a while haven't you, Alice?'

A stupid thrill goes through me at him saying my name like that. I'm so used to him calling me Ice Queen. What the hell is wrong with me? It must be his near nakedness. It's doing weird things to my brain.

He lays down on the pebble beach and immediately starts posing like Zoolander, pouting his lips ridiculously.

'Jesus, man, stop doing that.'

'What? You don't like my blue steel?' he asks, as if genuinely offended.

I roll my eyes. Jesus, I feel like I've been rolling them constantly since he's moved in. It's a wonder I haven't gone cross-eyed.

'I want you to look more natural.'

'These many muscles aren't natural,' he sniggers. 'I work bloody hard to look like this.'

He's so full of himself. 'What do you want me to do? Bow down to you?'

'Yep, and while you're down there.' He winks.

'Ugh! You're such a pig.'

'You love it,' he laughs. 'Okay, do you just want me to smile or what?'

I think about it for a second. 'No, try looking away from the camera and frowning. Maybe think about something that stresses you out.'

'Like what?' he asks.

'Jesus, for you it's probably two plus two! Just think about something.'

He pulls an excellent face, looking away as if in anguish.

'Perfect.' He moves subtly every few shots so I'm able to get an array of decent pictures. 'You're doing great.' I check back over the photos. They're looking good already. 'Okay, now I want you to look directly at the camera. Try to look intense.'

'It's fucking freezing,' he whinges, his teeth chattering.

'Just do it, Tom! The quicker we get this done, the quicker we can go.'

'You better make me the biggest cup of tea ever when we get home.'

It still feels weird him referring to my flat as home.

He closes his eyes for a second, opening them to stare down my camera lens, his green eyes so alive I feel a shiver down my spine. He looks like he wants to crawl over and take me, throw me down and ravish the fuck out of me. Shit, this guy's a good model.

I force myself to act non-affected and instead snap away. He's doing this for the photos, Alice. Not for you.

I look back at them. Shit, they're amazing. Brooke will definitely be able to sell these.

'Okay, great job. You can get dressed now.'

He walks over and slings on a t-shirt and hoodie he

brought with him. We start walking back towards the flat together.

'Those last few shots were great. They should show off our work well. What were you thinking of?' I can't help but ask.

He smiles at me from the side of his eyes. 'You naked.'

I'm so shocked, I stop dead in my tracks. 'What?' I blurt out, staring at him open mouthed.

He chuckles. 'Jesus, don't look so shocked. You've got a rocking little body.'

I don't know what I'm more shocked at. That he was thinking of me naked or that he just complimented me. But '*little body*'. How condescending.

'God, make up your mind,' I snap, choosing to channel my anger. 'First, you're calling me ugly, and then you're complimenting my body.'

He turns towards me, tilting his head to one side. 'Called you ugly? What the hell are you talking about?' He seems genuinely puzzled.

I feel myself turning bright red. I shouldn't have mentioned it. Now it looks like I give a shit what he thinks. When I don't. I bloody don't.

'The other day,' I admit on a sigh. I know he won't drop it until I tell him. 'You said I didn't have a pretty face.'

He frowns for a second before rolling his eyes. 'That was just a joke. Did you really think I was calling you ugly?'

I look down at the floor, embarrassed that I've shown him my insecure side.

'Hey.' He grabs my chin and forces it up, so I have to look at him. Into those amazing piercing greens. 'You are miles away from being ugly.'

I can't believe he's being serious for more than two seconds. For a minute, I wonder if he's going to kiss me.

He keeps looking down at my lips. Would I kiss him back? Should I kiss him back? Why the hell am I even imagining it?

'I'd totally bang you.'

And there he goes. Being the typical Tom 'Manwhore' Maddens I've come to expect.

'You're full of compliments today,' I scoff, removing his warm hand from my face.

He smirks. 'Oh, come on. You have to admit we're gonna do it soon.'

'Do *what* soon?' I shriek in horror. The boy's delusional.

'Have sex.' I stare back at him in disbelief. Is he this deluded? 'You know,' he continues, 'when a man and a woman go to bed together,' he explains like I'm a toddler. He starts doing hand motions. The idiot.

'I'm fully aware what sex is, thank you very much. But, I won't be having any with you. Not now, not soon, not ever. So, get that idea out of your head.'

'Okay,' he says, palms up in defeat. 'But I'll remind you of that when you're climbing me like a tree.'

Jesus, this guy's a dick.

Tom

I love how she acts like she doesn't want this. I saw her checking me out. She wants me and she knows it, but it's just her prissy little attitude that's holding her back. Don't get me wrong, I know deep down that I shouldn't be getting involved with someone I'm living with, but I eventually plan on getting a place of my own anyway. I can't be eating her veggie shit forever. So maybe we could fuck occasionally. And anyway, I want to prove Jack and Nic wrong.

But right now, I have bigger problems than trying to persuade Alice to fuck me. My new boss called me in today after work to thank me, just like I told Alice, but it wasn't the normal thank you. The bitch grabbed my dick through my trousers and asked if I'd liked to be really thanked.

I nearly shit my pants there and then. The woman's like twenty years older than me and married, not to mention ugly. I can't believe it. I finally get my dream life in Brighton, get to start afresh, and I have this pervert as my boss.

It was awkward as hell as my body reacted and started going hard. I had to push her away as politely as I could and explain that I think it better we just have a working relationship, but I could see it in her eyes; this isn't over. She wants me. Curse these good looks! Constantly getting me into trouble.

I'm just about to go to sleep when Charlie's name flashes up on my phone. Poor bastard probably misses me terribly. Especially with Jack now living here and Nicholas constantly back and forth.

'Hey, Charlie,' I say sleepily down the phone.

'Hey, man. I think I need your help.'

'Straight to the point,' I chuckle. 'Still hungover after birthday drinks, are you?'

He laughs. 'Nah, it was a quiet one. I'm saving it for the party Friday.'

'So, what's up?'

'Ugh, I need to lose some weight. I'm sick of being the fat mate.'

I roll my eyes even though he can't see me. 'Dude, you're not fat. But yeah, you do need to eat less shit. Just eat better food.'

He does this every year just around his birthday. Vows that he wants to lose weight and buff up. He normally lasts until November and then he starts eating mince pies.

'You know me, man. I need support. I need someone to tell me exactly what to eat and how to train.'

Just cut down on the McDonalds I want to say.

'So, what? You want me to make you a plan? I'm no personal trainer, dude.'

'Exactly. I can't afford one of those. You can do it for free.' He chuckles.

'Ah, I see. But...'

'But what?' he asks over eagerly.

I have to ask.

'You're not doing this for Molly, right? You're not still thinking you can bag her.'

The guy needs to get that she's into pussy.

He sighs. 'Will you guys shut up with that stuff? I know she's gay. I just want to lose weight and get healthier.'

'Okay,' I say, unconvinced. He's so got a crush on her. 'I'll do something and send it over in the next few days. Your email still charliewillywonkachocolatefactory?'

'Yep, that's me. Thanks, Tom! I owe you. See you at the party.'

Chapter 9

Friday 19th October

Alice

Today we've all got the day off work to drive up to Peter-borough. It was Charlie's birthday on Wednesday and his family have insisted on throwing him a birthday party, even though it's his thirty-second birthday. Apparently, they do it every year.

The lads told us it's because he's an only child and they absolutely dote on him. I think it's adorable. I'd love parents to be excited to celebrate the day I was born, but mine normally just invite me round for dinner so they can judge my life choices. That's something to look forward to in a month or so. I shudder just at the thought of it.

Tom's insisted on driving, claiming that I'm a shit woman driver. I only asked him to park my car on the road for me once. I'm not the best parallel parker at the best of times, and our road is filled up by six pm. Jack and Erica are in the car with us, while Brooke's taking Molly and Evelyn. I'm in the back with Erica, while the boys talk shit in the front.

'So, have you been missing home, Tom?' Erica asks him.

'I've barely been gone,' he chuckles. 'But, yeah, it'll be nice to see all of the lads together. But I've got to put up with the pussy harem.'

'Sorry?' I snort. 'Did you honestly just say the pussy *harem*? Who the hell do you think you are? Tom Hardy?'

I see him grin in the mirror. 'I have been compared to him.'

The annoying thing is that I can see that. He reminds me of him when he was younger and cleaner looking, before he got roughed up and utterly fuckable.

'But seriously, you think you have a little fan club here, do you?'

'Hey,' he snorts. 'I can't help that I'm in demand. Unfortunately, there's just not enough dick to go around.'

'I've heard there's just not enough dick,' Jack snorts. Tom reaches across and punches him playfully on the arm.

'You've been talking to some jealous exes, mate. They're all gagging for a bit of me.'

I roll my eyes. 'God, you are so self-assured. I can't wait to meet your parents. Find out what kind of idiots raised you.'

He grins. 'I think it's a bit too soon for you to be meeting the parents, sweetheart. I haven't even fucked you yet.'

Erica bursts out laughing. So not the supportive friend I'm looking for right now.

'Forget the 'yet' part of that sentence. You will *never* fuck me.' God, he's even got me talking like him.

He snorts. 'Prepare to eat your words, babe. That and my dick.'

'Oh my god, you are such a fucking pig!' I shout. 'I can't believe I'm being forced to live with you.'

'That's not what you said when you rang me up begging me to move in with you. I remember some pleading going on. You sounded pretty desperate for me. Get ready to be that desperate again, baby.'

Ugh, I despise when men call women 'baby'. Like we're some infant that's unable to look after themselves without a protective man. How pathetic. Everyone knows men wouldn't even exist if us women didn't experience the most excruciating pain imaginable to bring them into the world.

'You're right, I was desperate. As in, had no other choice as to how to make the rent.'

'God,' Jack laughs. 'You guys are like an old married couple.'

'Maybe you do need to sleep together,' Erica laughs. 'Just to get rid of this sexual tension.'

I glare at her. 'Just when I thought you'd be on my side, you go and say something stupid. There is no sexual tension between us. Just tension.'

Tom laughs. 'Well, maybe you should let me massage that tension right out of you.'

'Fuck off, Tom. Never gonna happen.' I rest my head against the window and close my eyes, purposely showing that I intend to go to sleep.

They all laugh like it's fucking hysterical. Dickheads. I'll be having words with Erica later. Just because she wants to go on loads of double dates, she wants us all to get with each other. Well, that's not how real-life works. And that's definitely not how Alice Watts works.

What the guys failed to tell us is that not only does Charlie's family celebrate with a party every year, but also that they enjoy embarrassing him by surprising him with a different childhood theme. This year it's a Batman party.

We're handed Batman masks as we enter the large village hall filled to the brim with black balloons, hanging bats and a huge sign on the wall that says 'Welcome to Gotham City. Happy birthday, Charlie.' There's a huge buffet table along one wall with buckets of beer in ice and a green punch called 'Joker Juice'.

'Help yourself to drinks,' a lady dressed as Joker says to us. Not a sexy Joker woman version like you're thinking. I'm talking the proper scary looking Heath Ledger version, and this is a woman in her early fifties.

The guys say hello and give her a kiss on the cheek.

'This is Charlie's Mum, Karen,' Jack shouts over the loud disco.

I stare back at the woman. Wow, she's really gone to town on her outfit. She's sprayed her hair bright green and drawn her red lipstick all the way to her ears. She has on a purple pin-stripe suit which looks at least a size too small. I'm expecting it to burst and to be blinded by a button any minute. Underneath, she has on a green shirt showing far too much cleavage, and a yellow waistcoat.

We wave our polite hellos. Molly spots us and comes running over. 'Oh my god, you've met Charlie's mum. Aren't his family hilarious and so sweet?'

'Yeah, they're something, for sure,' Erica says in my ear.

I decide to just throw myself into it and pour myself some of the Joker juice. Looks like I'm in for a weird night. Might as well embrace it.

I actually can't believe how loved Charlie is. At first, I found it weird for them to be throwing a children's themed party and obviously dressing up. I was really shocked when his Dad was dressed as Robin in very tight exposing lycra. Let's just say I could see everything. *Everything.*

But now that I've had time to chat to his family, I see how lovely and down to earth they are. Despite being an only child, he has over fifteen first cousins, some with kids of their own dancing around in little Batman outfits. Watching him interact with them all really warms my heart. They all seem super close. It makes me wish my family were like this.

I'm just at the bar getting a round in when I hear a gaggle of girls talking about Tom.

'You can't still want him, can you, Rachel?' one friend asks.

'Of course I do! I know it's crazy, but once you've had Tom 'Manwhore' Maddens, you can't go back to normal guys.'

'I totally agree,' another joins in. 'He's ruined me for other men.'

'Right!' another one cackles. 'It's like he injected some crazy juice into my veins or something. I mean, I have never, and I mean *never* come like that before in my life.'

'Amen, sister!' They all burst out laughing.

Jesus. I don't know what to be more surprised about— the fact Tom was right about all of these girls lusting over him, or the fact that he sounds amazing in bed. My past *very limited* experience has been that the more a guy is a slut, the worse he is in bed. He's never had to try hard, never had to please a long-term girlfriend. Just pumped and dumped. Gotten on with his life.

Now I know he's an orgasm master, well... I can't help

but think of him differently. Maybe with some newfound respect. No, shit, what am I thinking? I must have had too much of that Joker juice. I don't respect Tom. The guy's a pig. I decide to order shots instead.

I've just finished downing a second one when I'm approached by a tall slim guy with fair hair. He's good looking enough. Looks quite wholesome.

'Hi, I'm Charlie's cousin.' Of course he is, they all are. 'How do you know Charlie?'

'Oh, it's kind of a long story.' I'm too drunk right now to even start to begin about Jack and Erica being reunited on holiday and it having changed all our lives.

'I'd love to hear it sometime.' He grins, and I find myself blushing. Drunk Alice has not got game. 'I'm busy with family tonight, but maybe I could take your number and hear it another time?'

Oh, bless him. It's been a while since I've been chatted up. I open my mouth, just about to tell him thanks, but no thanks, that I actually live in Brighton, when I spot Tom staring at us both from across the room. His eyes are narrowed, his ears bright red. He seems furious. Why the hell would he be furious with me? I should give this guy my number, show Tom that I'm not the ugly little ducking he thinks I am.

'Yeah, okay,' I smile, taking his offered phone and putting in my name and number.

I awkwardly wave, spin on my heel and bring the tray of drinks back over to the table.

'Having fun there, Alice?' Charlie shouts over the music with a grin.

I feel myself turning bright red. Tom is glaring at me like I have the devil inside me. What is his fucking problem?

'Who wants to dance?' Brooke asks, clearly having sensed my awkwardness.

'Yes!'

We all pile onto the packed dance floor. Everyone is drunk enough now to shake their arses without feeling self-conscious. I'm dancing across from Brooke when I feel arms on my hips. I look at Brooke with wide eyes, praying for help from whoever is daring to touch me. She just grins and dances away from me.

I tense.

'Sssh,' they whisper in my ear. 'It's just me.' It's Tom's voice.

Tom has his hands on my waist and is dancing against me.

'It's just a dance, Ice Queen.'

I can't help it, I dance. Blame it on the Joker juice, or maybe the sexual tension that earlier I was sure was just plain tension, but before I know it, I'm pushing my arse back ever-so-slightly and grinding against him.

He places his head on my shoulder, with a pleasant view of my barely there cleavage. He's wasted too which helps me reassure myself that this is just a dance. It doesn't mean anything, and I won't be embarrassed tomorrow.

His hands wrap all the way around my waist. God, it feels good. It must be because I haven't been touched in a while. That and I'm desperate for an orgasm that I now know Tom could give me.

The song changes, and just as fast as he was here, he's gone, his weight no longer pressing against me. I turn to ask him what's up but freeze when I see him dancing exactly the same way with one of his fan club.

My heart sinks. I'm such a dickhead. Thinking for even a drunken moment that Tom 'Manwhore' Maddens might actually fancy me. Might actually be interested in more than a warm vagina to park his dick for the night.

I'm such a twat, and I can't help but feel completely humiliated in front of everyone. Even though everyone is pretty wasted and doesn't seem to have noticed, just knowing that for a fleeting moment I considered the possibility of me and him makes me feel stupid and dirty. I will never be a Maddens whore.

Chapter 10

Saturday 20th October

Alice

I stretch and squint my eyes, feeling the effects of the alcohol. It is true what they say, every year older it gets harder to handle hangovers. I focus my eyes and nearly jump out of my skin to see Brooke staring at me.

'Jesus, Brooke. Shit the life out of me, why don't you?'

She giggles. 'Sorry, but I've been waiting for you to wake up.'

'Why, what's up?' God, I need a coffee. Or six.

She rolls her eyes as if I should already be clued up on what she wants to talk about.

'I want to find out what's happening with Tom, of course. I saw how furious he was when you were being chatted up by Charlie's cousin.'

I sigh. 'Yeah, well he wasn't that bothered.'

'He looked it when he was grinding his dick into you.' She cackles, her really dirty cackle.

'Well, then you obviously missed him doing the exact same to nearly every girl in the room afterwards.'

She nods. 'Yeah, he is a total slag. But I just wanted to tell you that I get it.'

I look over her face for further explanation. 'Sorry, get what?'

'What it feels like to be into him. Knowing you're into a fuck boy and not being able to help it anyway.'

I sigh and roll away from her. It's too early for this shit. 'Fuck off, Brooke. I already put up with enough teasing from the others. I am not into Tom!'

'Okay, okay,' she laughs, rolling me back to her. 'All I'm saying is that it makes you no less of a confident, intelligent woman to fall for his charms.'

'Really?' I ask sarcastically. 'So that's why I felt like the biggest twat in the world for just letting him dance with me?'

'I knew you were gonna feel like this. Don't take it personally; this is just the game that Tom plays.'

'Yeah, well I don't want to play it. I'm not interested in him, or any man for that matter. I just want to focus on my career right now.'

She smiles, as if unconvinced. 'You keep telling yourself that, hun.'

Brooke's gone back with Molly and Evelyn. Erica and Jack stayed at his parents' house and are waiting with me by the hotel for Tom to pick us up. Thankfully, neither of them brings anything up. I think we're all too hungover, sipping from our coffee cups in harmonious silence. I'm looking forward to sleeping on the way back.

Tom's car rounds the corner and pulls up. It's only when he's getting out that I notice a woman is getting out of the passenger side too. It's the skank from last night, who's still in her party clothes with smudged mascara under her eyes. I cannot believe him. He literally cannot keep his dick in his pants.

'See you later, handsome,' she sings from a mouth full of smudged lipstick.

He smacks her arse. 'Later, sweet cheeks.'

It doesn't help that he looks gorgeous. All freshly showered with still damp hair and smelling amazing. Ugh, I must still be drunk.

'Unbelievable,' I mutter under my breath as I get into the back seat.

'I know I am, baby,' he says as he chucks my case into the boot.

I hate that he heard me.

I pull my scarf up over my ears, lean against the window, and pray for sleep.

***

Tom

I'm just getting our bags out of the boot after arriving back at Brighton when Jack pulls me to one side.

'Tom, I need a word.'

'Ohhkay,' I say with a grin. 'What's up?'

'I need to know what's going on with Alice?'

I scoff. 'Mate, I just fucked Crystal last night. Fuck all is going on with Alice.'

He raises his eyebrows in that way he does when he knows I'm bullshitting. 'Tom, I saw you last night. First at how fucking jealous you were when Charlie's cousin was chatting her up, and then when you were dancing with her. If you can call it dancing. Jesus, Tom, it was a family party and there you were grinding into her like we were in the middle of a club.'

I roll my eyes. 'It was just a dance. No big deal.'

'Maybe not to you, Tom. But I know Alice better than you. Hell, I know women better than you.'

'Sure you do, bud,' I interrupt sarcastically.

'And believe me when I say that you can't fuck with them like this. Leading them on one minute and then going off to fuck Crystal the next. You're playing a dangerous game.'

'Oh, chill out, Jack.' He can be such a woman sometimes.

'No,' he snaps. 'I won't chill out. If you end up sleeping with Alice and then treating her like shit, it's going to fuck up the whole group dynamic.'

I roll my eyes. 'You're being dramatic.'

'Am I?' he sneers. 'Because I can't see how Erica's going to let me be friends with you when you've broken her best friend's heart.'

'Did you just say *let you* be friends with me? Fuck, Jack, you're whipped.'

'No, Tom, I'm in love. And I won't let anything get in the way of that, especially not you. This is a warning.'

'Hey, if I want to go after Alice I will.'

'Fine,' he barks. 'But if you do, know that she wants a relationship. She's not like you. Only do it if you want one too, or you're fucking with her before you even start. I mean it, Tom.'

He turns and storms off. Well, someone started their period this morning.

Alice

I managed to ignore Tom all the way home by pretending to be asleep. I then went straight to my room and straight to sleep for a good few hours. When I woke up, he'd gone out. I decided I was going to try to clear the air. Or better yet, pretend nothing ever happened. So, I've made us a vegetable casserole that smells amazing.

I'm just editing Tom's photos on my laptop—which Brooke is chasing me for—when I hear him come in. He's a noisy fucker at the best of times (I blame his size) but tonight I hear a strange sort of scuttling coming from the hallway. I'm just carrying the vegetable casserole from the kitchen over to the table when suddenly a puppy rounds the corner. What the fuck?

Before I can register why the hell it's in my apartment it jumps up at me. I back away, not wanting its claws to mark my bare legs, but in doing so manage to trip over it. How the hell did it get back underneath my legs again? I try my hardest to remain upright, but I fall backwards, the casserole pot flying from my arms.

'Shiiiiit!' I shriek, landing flat on my back, hot sauce splashing me on the face. I'm lucky the dish didn't smash on me.

I wipe my eyes clean with the back of my hand, so I can open my eyes. Thank God, it wasn't hot enough to scald me. When I do open them, I see Tom leaning over me holding a Jack Russell in his arms.

'So, you met Pickles then?' he asks with a shit-eating grin.

I glare back at him, every muscle in my body quivering with rage. 'What the fuck is going on?'

He reaches out his hand for me to take. The dog tries to spring free from the other one.

'Aargh! Keep that dog away from me,' I shriek, crawling backwards away from him. I've never liked dogs. They're so unpredictable.

He rolls his eyes. 'Not *that* dog. *Our* dog.'

I reluctantly take his hand and help him take me to standing. I look around to see that the casserole dish is smashed on the floor and the dog is struggling to get out of Tom's arms to lick it up. Ew.

'Tom, don't fuck with me right now. I just spent the best part of forty-five minutes cooking that and now you're talking a load of nonsense.'

He passes me a tea towel, so I can clean my face. Turns out I had a lot more on there than I thought. This is going to take ages to wash out of my hair.

He rests himself against the back of the sofa. 'Okay, I'll talk slowly. This is our new puppy, Pickles.'

I wipe myself down as best I can, knowing I'll have to just throw myself in the shower.

'You bought a puppy?' Even my voice sounds like it's given up.

'Yes,' he nods with raised eyebrows as if I'm slow. 'For us. I've called him Pickles.'

There's so much wrong with that, I really don't know where to start.

I sigh, sitting down on the chair. 'Okay, first of all you bought a puppy without consulting me? And second, you decided to call him fucking Pickles?'

He smiles down at the dog as if it's the greatest thing in the world. It stares up back at him in wonder.

'Yes. I was just down the pub for a quick pint and there was a guy in there selling him.'

I frown, a migraine coming on. 'Sorry, you bought a puppy from a random fucking guy in the pub? He's probably from one of those awful puppy farms. Don't get too attached, he'll probably be dead within the week. Full of disease.'

He covers the puppy's ears, as if he can understand me. Soppy bastard.

He smiles sadly at Pickles. 'I couldn't just leave him there. The guy looked homeless. He wasn't safe with him.'

'So, you decided to bring him here?' I ask incredulously. I really can't believe this guy. How has he got so far without a brain?

'Yeah,' he shrugs. 'I've always wanted a dog, but my parents always said no.'

'Because they have sense!' I shout, making Pickles cower under Tom's arm. 'Did you honestly think I'd be cool with this?'

'Yes!' He stares back at me as if I'm a monster. 'What couldn't you love about a dog? The walks, the cuddles, the companionship? There are literally no downsides.'

'Err, the dog shit, the drooling, the barking, the being tied to the house?' I say, counting it out on my fingers. 'I can think of quite a few, and that's only off the top of my head.'

He rolls his eyes. 'Jesus, you're so negative. You need some puppy love.' He pushes the puppy into my face. It looks at me with his head turned to the left. It is kind of cute.

'Well, make the most of it tonight, because I'm taking it back tomorrow.'

He flinches, taking the puppy back under his arm. 'You can't! He's our baby.'

What's with this *our* thing?

'He's a bloody dog and he shouldn't be living in a flat. Take him somewhere else in the morning, Tom. I mean it.'

He plonks the dog down on my chest, forcing me to scramble to hold him. 'Fine, but you have to be the one to tell him.'

I wake at two am to crying. What the hell is that? It's so high-pitched, it can't be Tom. Ah, that's when I remember the puppy. Can a thing that small seriously make that much noise? I stumble out of bed, open my door and follow the sound into Tom's room. I go in unannounced, presumably looking like death, to find Pickles on the bed with Tom who's in a right mess. He looks like he hasn't slept a wink—his hair in disarray, and his eyes heavy.

'What the hell is wrong with him?' I shriek to a sleepy Tom.

'God knows.' He yawns. 'Since you've gone to bed, he won't stop crying.'

I pick him up. 'What the hell is wrong with you, Pickles?'

He starts licking my face. God, he's annoying.

'He's quietened down since you've arrived.'

'Well, unfortunately I can't sleep in here.' I look at his exhausted eyes and can't help but feel bad for him. 'Look, I'll take him for the next hour or so. Let you get some sleep.'

'Oh my god, thank you!' he says, so grateful. 'I could kiss you.'

No need to make it awkward, Tom.

I take him into my room. The minute I'm away from Tom, he starts whining again. Ugh. I place him on my chest, so he can hear my heartbeat, hoping it'll soothe him. It does to a certain extent, but he keeps glancing forlornly at the door with a whimper. He misses Tom? He's literally only just come away from him.

I manage to snooze lightly when I'm suddenly woken by Tom. He shakes my shoulder softly.

'Hey, Alice.'

I open my eyes, the puppy still on my chest, but now with his tail whipping me in the face and him whimpering again. I spit out the dog's hairs that have made their way into my mouth.

'I think he just wants to be with both of us.'

'Ugh, then get in,' I growl. Anything is worth a try at this point. I'm so fucking tired.

He peels back the cover and gets in. Pickles circles himself around at the end of the bed before collapsing silently.

'He's asleep,' he whispers in shock and awe. 'Shall I risk sneaking out?'

'Just stay there,' I snap, completely exhausted. It's just easier. 'If you wake him again I'll fucking murder you.'

Chapter 11

Sunday 21st October

Alice

I wake up to Tom's face squished in my neck. How the hell he managed to fit his entire mush in there I don't know. Plus, he's snoring. I push him away from me. He snorts but doesn't wake. It's funny how he looks almost angelic when he's unconscious. His skin is still tanned as if he just walked off Luna Island beach. I wonder if he does more than sunbeds. Maybe fake tan. I'll have to raid his room when he's out.

I look down at Pickles. He's still at the bottom of the bed but stirs slightly when he notices me. He stretches his little body out, yawning. It's the cutest thing I've ever seen. He forces himself up and walks on over to me, almost collapsing at every dip in the duvet.

'Morning, Pickles,' I whisper, so as not to wake Tom. I don't know what time it is, but his alarm hasn't gone off yet. It's loud and obnoxious so I can normally hear it from here.

Pickles starts licking my face, but in doing so his little

tail whips against Tom's cheek. He wakes up, immediately greeted by Pickles' arse and screams.

Pickles yelps and jumps off the bed, running towards the door.

'Way to scare the puppy,' I snort.

He looks at me, as if completely mystified that he's in the same bed as me. 'Huh?'

'Earth to Tom. You just scared the dog.' I stretch out, conscious not to touch him. 'You never warned me that this dog was going to be like a baby. I'm wrecked.'

He yawns, his biceps stretching over his head. 'They don't tell you this when you buy them.'

'This is why they sell them to idiots,' I say with a smile, turning to face him.

My phone beeps with a text message. I open it up to see a number I don't recognise.

Hi, Alice. It's Charlie's cousin Alfie. I work in London and wondered if you fancied meeting up sometime for a drink?

'Who is it?' Tom asks, trying to peer over my shoulder.

'No one,' I insist, feeling my cheeks blush. I never actually thought the guy would contact me.

'Let me see,' he insists, grabbing the phone from my hand.

'No! Tom!' I shout, frantically running around after him in my room.

'Whoa, wait. That idiot Alfie texted you?'

'So?' I shrug, crossing my arms over my chest.

'So, are you going to go out with him?'

I shrug again. 'I don't know.'

His face drops. He looks down at Pickles. 'I better let him out for a wee.'

I watch from my bed as he gets his jacket and starts to

carry him out. 'Are you going in just your boxer shorts?' I shout after him.

'Yep. Too tired to give a shit right now.'

I watch him through the window as he walks into the communal gardens and waits for him to do his toileting. Everyone is curtain-twitching to see who the semi-naked man in the garden is. Not that he seems to care. He's seriously comfortable being naked. Not that he shouldn't be. The guy is ridiculously stacked.

I can't believe I let him sleep in here with me. Not that I still think he's sick enough to grope me or anything, but my god, what being bone-tired will make you do.

I stare down at the message from Alfie. Should I text him back? The sad thing is that the only man stuck in my head right now is Tom 'Manwhore' Maddens. The arrogant prick.

With me returning Pickles today, we'll be able to sleep in our own beds tonight. Only... God, is it mad that I kind of liked having Tom there? No, I'm just severely sleep deprived and starting to lose my mind. But... well in this cold it's nice to have a warm body pressed against you.

Tom

Well, waking up with a boner was awkward. Thank God she didn't seem to notice. Or maybe she was too polite to mention it. Luckily, I could use the excuse of Pickles needing to go outside to shock my dick back to normal with the cold.

But damn, being that close to Alice and her amazing scent, it was just too much. Even in my exhausted state, I couldn't help but discreetly sniff her. She smells of marshmallows and dark chocolate. I can't remember seeing her eating that, so it must be her perfume. What a weird, but totally intoxicating choice.

I can't believe she's giving that boring dickwad Alfie a chance. The guy's dull as fuck. She needs someone that's going to challenge her. Really get under her skin.

Another thing I forgot about was having to pick up dog shit. I can hardly just leave it there, what with all the neighbour's curtains twitching. I hope they don't report us to the landlord. I mean, for all I know we could be banned from having pets larger than a hamster.

Without a bag, I have to resort to plucking some leaves and using them to scoop it up. Ugh, how I don't vomit I don't know. I rush back in, Pickles in one arm and the poo in the other. I flush it down the loo as soon as I can.

Jesus. What the hell have I brought on myself? Maybe Alice was right about returning him.

Alice

So, after a quick shower to wake myself up I'm headed to the pub with this puppy. I'm trying not to call him Pickles. That would get me feeling attached to him. I mean, yes, every time I look into his deep brown eyes my heart throbs full of love, but that's not going to stop me. No way. The thing kept me awake all night. Nothing comes between me and my sleep.

I get to the pub as soon as it opens and quiz the manager, Liz, about the homeless guy selling a dog.

'Hmm,' she scratches her head, eyebrows bunched together. 'There wasn't a homeless guy, but there was a woman talking to him. She gave him a card.'

A woman? I'd have definitely remembered if he'd have said it was a normal woman.

'Wait, are you sure? No homeless guy with this dog?' I point down to him as if it'll jog her memory.

'I'm pretty sure I'd remember,' she nods, trying and failing to hide a smirk. 'He ended up leaving with her. I picked up the card actually.' She walks over to the bin behind the bar and opens the lid. 'Ah, I thought so. Here it is.' She reaches in, grabs it and gives it to me.

I look down at the card covered in fag ash. Jean Mackenna, Dog Breeder.

Dog breeder? He made out he bloody rescued the thing! Not bought it from some breeder.

There's an address here. I thank the woman and head straight for the car. I place the puppy on the front seat next to me and enter the address into the Sat Nav.

Within twenty-five minutes I pull up to a farm. This looks like it. As soon as I get out of the car, the sound of dogs barking overwhelms my ears. Jesus, there must be at least twenty dogs here.

I follow the raucous noise to an outdoor kennels with newborn puppies separated from their mother. I thought they were supposed to be kept together at this age?

'Hello?' a woman says behind me. 'Can I help you?'

I spin around with a forced smile. 'Oh, yes, I'm looking for Jean Mackenna.'

She smiles revealing a cracked front tooth. 'That's me.'

Definitely not a homeless guy. She's tall, blonde, and wearing muddy wellies. Maybe in her late-thirties to early-forties.

'Ah, well, my roommate bought this puppy from you yesterday and I wanted to return it.'

She looks down at the dog in my arms who's trying to

snuggle into my neck. Oh, sleepy *now* are you? You little shit.

Her smile quickly vanishes. 'Sorry, no returns. If you don't want it, take it to the dog shelter. It's too old to sell now.'

My mouth drops open in shock at her attitude. 'Are you serious? How could you see a puppy go to a place like that?'

She leans on one hip. 'Look, you're not getting your £750 back,' she snaps.

He spent £750 on a dog? Jesus, think of the shoes you could buy with that kind of money! Does that mean he's going to be short on his first month's rent? I'll kill him with my bare hands!

'The dog is already sixteen weeks. Do you know how old that is in puppy time? She's had her vaccinations too. I practically gave her away.'

Yeah, right. For £750 bloody pounds.

I have to think of a new tactic. Some way of getting her to accept him back.

'To be honest with you, Tom, well, he has difficulties, if you know what I mean?'

She frowns. 'Difficulties? I don't follow.'

'He has *learning difficulties*,' I explain on a whisper with a sad smile. 'Sometimes he has the mind of a seven-year-old. I'm actually his carer.'

I'm going to hell.

'God, poor love,' she says, nodding in understanding. 'He did make some inappropriate jokes. I just thought he was a bit of a pig.'

I bite my tongue to stop myself laughing. 'Because he's such a big strong guy people assume he's fine.'

She frowns, chewing on her lip. 'Either way, I'm sorry, but I still can't give you your money back. I can take back the dog, but she'll probably end up in a dog shelter.'

I look down at the dog snuggled up next to me and then back at the kennels of barking dogs. He seems too small and fragile. What if he has a nervous breakdown? I wouldn't be able to sleep knowing I'd done that. Not that I'll sleep if I keep him.

'I don't know. Is his mother still here?'

'Yeah, she's in there.'

I look over into the cage she's pointed at to see a dog with terribly swollen teats. It's obvious she's been over-bred. This is such a puppy farm. My heart bleeds for her.

'Aren't the puppies still supposed to be with her at this stage?' I probe.

She scoffs. 'They're sixteen weeks. And who are you? The police?'

The fact she's so defensive proves she knows she's in the wrong.

'No, but I'm just a bit worried about them.'

Her face instantly hardens. 'Listen, you let me worry about them. Now, do you want me to take the dog back or not?'

'Not.' I turn and head back to the car. There is no way I'm giving him to that awful lady. I pull away while asking Siri to call the RSPCA for me. Someone needs to report this bitch.

I took Pickles to the vet to get him checked over. After seeing the conditions in which he was brought into the world, I was worried he'd be riddled with disease. You hear about this sort of thing all the time. The puppies are mass-produced without time for the mother to rest, and then they're sold off to the highest bidder. How that woman can live with herself I don't know.

Well, first of all it turns out he's a she. Tom mustn't have stopped to look for a doggy penis. Something which shocks me.

While I was there, I got her chipped and so had to give her a name for their records. Pickles it is. Bloody ridiculous name that is, but now that I look at her she sort of suits it. The vet estimated that she's about sixteen weeks, so that corroborates with what she told me. He said he'd heard of the woman and knew what vets she went to. He's going to give them a call and double check that she's had all her jabs.

When I get home, Tom's already there. He looks worried about my reaction, chewing on his lip and pacing the floor. Obviously he knows by now I'd have found out he was lying about the homeless guy. His eyes widen in surprise when he sees Pickles is still with me.

I calmly place Pickles in Tom's arms and then slam down an invoice. 'You owe me £20 for her chip. You also need to order her a collar, name tag, and all the rest of that dog crap.'

His eyes brighten with hope. 'You mean... we can keep him?' he asks apprehensively.

I roll my eyes. 'First of all, Pickles is a *girl*, not a boy. And, well... I mean that we're stuck with her. The *woman* you bought her from won't give you your money back.'

His eyes widen in alarm. Sometimes his face is so readable it's embarrassing.

'Yes, that's right. I know it wasn't a homeless man. Why fucking lie, Tom?'

He sighs, running his hand through his hair. 'Because I knew you'd be far more likely to let her stay if you thought she was a cute little orphan.'

My nostrils flare. *Try not to kill him. You'll go to prison. You won't do well there.*

'Yeah, well the place is a shit hole. There's no way I'd send her back there. What the hell were you thinking getting a dog from a blatant puppy farm like that?'

He shrugs. 'It just all happened so quickly. First, I was chatting to her, then she mentioned dogs and invited me back to hers. I thought I was getting lucky and then she took me into the kennels. I was about to leave when I saw Pickles. She looked so sad. I just couldn't leave her there.'

He's a right soppy bastard really. A big muscled, stupid, soppy bastard.

'Yeah, but £750, Tom? How the hell do you have that kind of money?'

'Savings,' he shrugs. 'All gone now though.'

'Well you better start saving up sharpish, pretty boy, because dogs are expensive. And you need insurance.'

'Yeah,' he sighs, running his hand through his hair. 'Maybe, I didn't think all this through?'

'Yeah, no shit, Sherlock. Plus, you'd better be able to still pay rent or you're out on your arse.'

He nods. 'I can still pay rent.'

I sigh. 'The only other option is to send her to a dog's home and we can't do that.'

'God, no.' He cuddles Pickles close. 'You're not going anywhere, are you?' he says in a weird baby voice.

'God, you're manly,' I deadpan. 'And what the hell made you come up with the awful name of Pickles?'

'I just think it suits him.' He shakes his head. 'I mean her. Anyway, I'll get on with ordering that lead.'

'No rush on that,' I scoff. 'You can't walk her until we know she's had all of her jabs.'

'What?' he shrieks, his jaw open. 'The whole point of

getting a dog was to walk it. Now you're telling me I have to wait until I can?'

I roll my eyes. 'Yes, bimbo, you have to be patient. That'll teach you a lesson for rushing into it. These things are as much of a commitment as a baby. Have you even thought about where she's going to be during the day while you're at work?'

'Here with you?' he shrugs.

Unbelievable. *Murder sends you to prison. You'll never become a fashion photographer with a criminal record.*

'Have you forgotten that I actually work too? I know I'm freelance, but I do need to leave the house to do photo shoots.'

He shrugs. 'Jack said your work had dried up recently.'

The hairs on the back of my neck stand up. Does that mean Jack's told him about the photos? I'll fucking kill him if he has.

'I'm still working, Tom. I haven't retired.'

'Then just take her with you. She can't cause that much trouble. Everyone loves puppies, right?'

Famous last words.

Chapter 12

Monday 22nd October

Alice

Another night of that goddamn dog crying at all hours. This time I ended up crawling into Tom's bed. I'm actually starting to get desensitized to sleeping with him, and worse yet, liking the heat of his body against mine. I blame the wintry weather.

First thing, I'm googling *how to stop your puppy crying in the night*. I'm bombarded by information about crate training, clothes that smell of you, toys with heartbeats in them, and everything in between.

It's giving me a headache just thinking about it. I storm into the kitchen, pissed beyond belief that Tom's put this on me. It was hard enough getting a roommate and now I'm stuck with a dog too.

I turn the kettle on, desperate for a coffee. Something to shift this shit mood I'm in.

'Good morning,' Tom says, wiping the sleep out of his eyes as he walks into the kitchen carrying Pickles.

Damn it, what is it about a big burly man carrying a small dog that has me feeling all tingly? It must be the lack of sleep doing strange things to my mind. That's all his fault.

'Is it?' I snap back, gritting my teeth.

His eyes widen. 'Okay. I'm guessing you didn't get much sleep last night.'

I'm too exhausted to even roll my eyes. 'We have to get this sorted. I can't be living like this. I feel like I have a newborn baby, for Christ's sake.'

He grimaces. 'Yeah, I'll admit I didn't exactly see it panning out like this.'

At least he's big enough to admit when he's wrong.

'Yeah, well you wouldn't, because you only ever think about things for two seconds. Unless it involves your dick.'

My eyes betray me by looking down at it bulging through his boxer shorts. Dang, he's well endowed. No wonder he's such a cocky bastard with that concealed weapon.

He catches me looking and smirks. 'My eyes are up here,' he says pointing dramatically to his face.

'Oh, shut up, Tom.' I feel my cheeks burning. I turn to watch the kettle.

'Maybe you're right.'

I stare back at him, dumbfounded. 'I'm... I'm right? Sorry, what?'

He must be bloody sleep deprived if he's telling me I'm right. It's not his style to admit defeat so easily.

He sighs, putting Pickles down onto the floor. 'Maybe we should give her to a rescue centre.'

My mouth drops open. 'Tom! You can't just abandon her just because you're a frigging idiot. You know how over-run those places are. She could be in there for months, years even.'

He sits down at the kitchen table, his head in his hands.

'I'm just so fucking tired. I have no idea how I'm going to work today.'

'Me either,' I nod. I can't help but look at Pickles drinking out of her water bowl. If she was ugly, this would be so much easier.

His eyebrows move inwards towards each other. 'You're not working today, are you?'

'Yeah,' I nod, eyebrows furrowed. 'Why wouldn't I be?' Since when has he been following my work schedule?

'I looked at the calendar.' He walks over to it. 'You've got nothing written down.'

Jesus, since when did we become a married couple? I don't have to check in with him.

'Yes, I have. I wrote it in my handbag diary. I didn't realise I had to confirm with you.' I snort a laugh.

'Jesus, woman. How many diaries do you need? Can't you go digital like the rest of the world?'

I glare back at him. 'I don't know if you noticed, but I don't like to follow the mass crowd.'

He snorts. 'You can say that again.'

Grr, it's okay when I say it. Not when he says it. Dickhead.

'But I thought you'd be able to look after her. Your job is flexible, right? You can bring her along?'

Is he serious? 'No, I bloody can't. My jobs are just as important as yours.'

'Well then, she'll just have to stay here on her own. I'm already on thin ice at work. If I try to sneak a puppy in, they'll fire me for sure.'

What the hell is he talking about? He's never mentioned this before.

'Thin ice? Why are you on thin ice?'

He avoids my eye-line, choosing instead to stare down

at the table. 'It's a long story, but at the end of the day, I can't bring her in to work with me.'

At the end of the day, he's still an arse hat and yet again it's all down to me.

'Oh, and did you ever get back to Alfie?'

Alfie? Oh, he means Charlie's cousin. Why's he so interested?

'Nah. I don't think he's my type.'

He nods, turns and mutters 'good' under his breath.

So that's how I find myself taking this mad dog for a walk before my appointment at a low budget fashion magazine, after getting the thumbs up from the vets that she's had all her vaccinations. That way, I figure if I tire her out, she'll just sleep through the interview. She's only small. How much bloody energy can she have?

I take her to the open park and watch all the well-behaved dogs running off-lead. I look down at her walking, pulling eagerly against the lead. She looks back at me with a smile. Well, what I think is a smile. I mean, who knows if dogs actually smile.

If I let her off-lead it would be a quick way to burn off some energy. I bought a bag full of treats on the way here, so I know I can tempt her back.

Oh, fuck it. I unclip her and watch as she runs into the middle of all the dogs, her energy surprising me. I didn't think that was possible anymore. She starts playing with them, bouncing off them like she's on a trampoline.

Well, this is an easy way to get her to burn off some of that puppy energy. She's been playing freely for thirty minutes when my phone starts ringing with a withheld number.

'Hello?' I answer dubiously.

'Hi, Miss Watts. This is PC Edwards.'

'Oh, hi.'

'I'm just calling to let you know that we've seized Mr Cundy's computer, and it's been sent to high-tech crime.'

'Okay, great. How was he?' I can't help but ask. 'Ted, I mean. Did he seem angry? Do you think I'm going to get any repercussions?' That's the last thing I need.

'He was defensive, but I doubt you will. If you do, please call me straightaway. In the meantime, I'm afraid that it could take some weeks before high-tech crime find something we can use. I just wanted to keep you updated.'

I thank him and hang up, keeping a close eye on Pickles.

I watch as the dogs leave the park one by one. When there are just a few dogs left, I call her over.

'Pickles!' I shout, patting my thighs like I've seen all the other owners do.

She turns to look at me, but then carries on playing.

I walk a bit closer. 'Pickles! Home time.'

Again, she looks before running slightly further away, playing with the two remaining dogs. The little bitch. This isn't going how I planned.

I walk right up to her, trying to remain calm and not look worried in front of the other confident dog walkers. They're confident because they have well-behaved dogs. Pickles seems to stay where she is. Oh, thank God, she's co-operating. I manage to walk straight up to her and I'm about to attach her collar to the lead when she bolts again. For fuck's sake!

'PICKLES!' I roar, stomping off after her. I can feel the dog walkers looking on in judgement. 'She's a puppy,' I offer pathetically, as a way of an explanation. My heart is beating out of my chest and my neck is sticky with sweat.

Every time I go towards her she runs further away. Right, maybe a bit of reverse psychology could work here. It's worth a try. Anything is worth a try at this point.

'I'm going home now, Pickles. Bye!' I turn and walk away, praying to God she's following me. I walk a few more steps before glancing around to see she hasn't moved at all.

Shit. She couldn't care less.

The two owners call their dogs back and like perfect little things they trot off to them and allow themselves to be put back on the lead. Pickles looks on and for a moment I think she's going to copy them.

I straighten my spine, a new confidence in me. 'Pickles,' I call calmly, copying how they stoop down to the dog.

She starts walking towards me. Oh my god, she's coming towards me. It's working. Thank the Lord.

But... then she turns and fucks off again.

UGH!

This is a disaster. I should have never taken her off the lead. This must be on page one of *Puppy Disasters to Avoid*. I really need to order that book.

'Pickles!' I look into my pocket to get the treats out. Fuck, I must have left them in the car. Fuck my life.

Instead I find a half-eaten packet of vegan chocolate biscuits. I take it out in desperation, crinkling the packet, hoping the noise alone will get her back.

She turns from a distance, tilts her head to the left, and comes bounding over. Yes! It's working! Thank God. My heart rate is already returning to normal. This is fine. She's going to eat a vegan biscuit and while she's doing that, I'll grab her by the collar and put her back on the lead.

She's just about to get to me when she stops mid step, her left foot stopped in front of her. Wait, is she on to me?

Two men enter the park from the other end with two

other dogs. They throw a ball for them and that's it, Pickles is off to try to get it. Grr, this dog is so dumb!

I make my way over to her as quickly as I can, my pits so sweaty I'm worried the marks are going to go through my top. By the time I get to her, I see that she's stolen the ball from the dogs. Oh, for goodness' sake!

Now they're chasing her around the park to try to get it back. The dogs could kill her if she stops, but she seems oblivious, running with abandon, her mouth open in glee, her tail wagging.

'Sorry!' I shout as I walk hurriedly over to them, my calves burning. This is the most exercise I've done in years. 'I can't seem to get her back on the lead.' I admit, feeling a fool.

'You tried treats, love?' one asks, eyeing me up like the idiot I am.

Does he think I'm an imbecile? Well, look at me right now. Probably.

'Of course. She's just like a dog possessed.'

'We'll try to help.' He pulls out another ball and throws it in the air as if to entice her. She stops what she's doing and turns to watch him, as if entranced.

She keeps the ball in her mouth but moves towards him. He throws it up in the air again but when it falls to the floor, he quickly covers it with his foot. She tries to get it out, lowering her guard for a second. He grabs her by the collar.

'Got her!' he says triumphantly. Thank the Lord.

'Thanks!' I take her collar, and kneel down to attach the lead, but she suddenly bolts. Before I have a split second to register what's happening, I'm being dragged on my knees across the field in the mud. It burns.

I force myself to let go so that my neck isn't broken. I land face down in the mud. Little motherfucker! I'm going to kill her. She's gonna wish she made it to the animal shelter when I get hold of her.

I look up to see her at the opposite side of the park, looking back at me as if laughing. That little satanic bitch. She's finding this funny. And this is the little dog I couldn't see going to a dog shelter. She doesn't know how good she's got it.

I look back to the men. They cringe, as if not sure whether to ask if I'm okay or try to pretend like they didn't see it.

'I can't believe her,' I shriek, attempting an ironic laugh, when really, I just want to burst into tears. I force my tired limbs up to standing, the mud having gone underneath my nails. How humiliating.

'It's alright, love. I'll try again,' one of them says kindly, again trying to entice her with the ball.

That little bitch. Right now, if I ever get her back, I'm dragging her home and never letting her out again. And to think I'm against animal cruelty.

The man again throws the ball in the air, drops it to the floor but quickly stands over it. Pickles goes to get it, but this time the man practically jumps on her, rugby tackling her to the ground.

'I have her!' he shouts.

I rush over with the lead, my frantic fumbling hands barely able to attach her lead to the collar. Once it's attached, the relief is all consuming. I could cry. I feel as if I owe these men my life.

I stand up before she can try to drag me across the park again.

'Thank you so much. I really don't know what's gotten into her.' A traitorous tear slips out.

They exchange a glance which I think says *poor silly cow* and then they're on their way.

I drag her back to the car, cursing under my breath. The urge to lock her in a dark cupboard is strong, but I won't let her push me. I won't be turned into one of those mental people you see on those RSPCA programmes that have six dogs in cages full up of their own poo. No, I'm a fucking vegetarian for God's sake.

I love animals. I love animals. I repeat it to myself over and over again all the way to the car.

With her safely in the boot, I let myself into the driving seat and allow myself a minute to collect my wits. I rest my head down onto the steering wheel and take a deep breath. It's fine, Alice. No one died. No one got injured. Well, apart from me. My knees are throbbing from the grass burn of being dragged and my hands are slightly grazed. Just what a photographer needs.

I check my phone to see a text from Tom.

'Have a great morning. I'll pop home for lunch. Cook us something nice ;-)'

Gah, this bloody man!

Chapter 13

Tom

I throw my keys down onto the hallway console table.

'Hello?' I call. 'Anyone home?'

Maybe she didn't get my text. Then I hear some sort of scraping. Pickles rounds the corner, skidding so far she hits the wall, before continuing to barrel towards me.

'Hey, Pickles.' I pick her up, trying to stop her from licking my entire face. I don't doubt she's been licking her arse today. 'Have you been a good girl for Mummy?'

I make my way to the kitchen/diner, but instead of finding Alice in an apron (okay and in my imagination nothing else), about to serve me a replenishing lunch, she's instead sat at the table with her head in her hands.

Uh-oh. I look down at Pickles. What the hell did she do to her? She stares back with wide-eyed innocence, tilting her head to the left.

'Alice?'

She looks up, mud marring her forehead. Her hair is dishevelled from where it looks like she's run her hands through it and her eyes are red and puffy. My stomach drops at the idea of her being hurt.

'Have you been crying?' I rush over to her, placing Pickles on the floor.

She sniffs, but quickly attempts to pull herself together, chin in the air in defiance. 'No!'

She stands up and walks towards the fridge. It's only then I see the bottom half of her jeans are covered in mud, her knees grass-stained. I look down at Pickles. *What did you do?*

'Egg on toast?' she offers meekly, not meeting my eyes, choosing instead to hide her face in the fridge.

'Fuck the lunch,' I say, taking her hand and guiding her back to the table. 'What the hell's happened?'

I crouch down to her eye level.

'I've just... I've just had a shit day, that's all.' Her cheeks are all flushed, her chin wobbling. I can't help but find her captivating.

'Because of Pickles?' I finish for her. 'I'm assuming she wasn't the easy breeze I thought she'd be?'

'No,' she sobs, tears spilling thick and fast from her eyes. 'And... I just don't know if I can cope looking after her.'

'Hey.' I place my hand over hers in what I hope is a reassuring action. 'It can't be that bad.'

She scoffs. 'Ha!'

Oh dear. Underestimating a woman in this kind of situation is how men get killed.

'Start at the beginning. Tell me,' I plead, trying to meet her eyes.

She looks up at me with her big almond-shaped, pale-green eyes. I've never seen them look so vulnerable. This can't really all be about a dog, can it?

First, she explains about Pickles being a bitch at the park. I look down at her knees, knowing I need to look at them in case they're grazed.

'And then I went on to my meeting. I had to go like this because she'd already made me late.'

I stand up, take my jacket off, and roll up my sleeves. 'Take them off,' I say indicating to the jeans.

Her mouth hangs open. 'Ex- excuse me? Are you seriously hitting on me right now?'

Wait... she thinks...? I burst out laughing.

I smirk. 'Alice, if I wanted to hit on you I wouldn't just be ordering you to take your jeans off. I'd have at least thrown a compliment your way first.'

She smiles meekly, her cheeks turning pink. Wait, is she embarrassed that I'm not hitting on her? Chicks are so fucking complicated.

'I want to check your knees out. See if they're grazed.'

She looks down at them. 'Oh.'

She tries to roll them up first, but just as I thought, with how skinny those jeans are it's an absolute nightmare. Instead she reluctantly stands, undoes the button and wiggles them down her milky legs.

Do not get a boner, Tom. Now is not the right moment to get a boner.

I kneel down and take a look at them, trying to ignore her black lacy French knickers. One is fine, just a bit red, but her right-sided one is grazed, the skin ever so slightly ripped. I head to the kitchen sink to run a bit of kitchen roll under the cold tap.

'Anyway,' she continues a sigh. 'So, I go to this meeting, and I'm scared to leave her in the boot in case someone calls pet services on me or something. So, I ask the receptionist and she says it's fine, they're dog friendly.' She rolls her eyes as if to tell me they're not that dog friendly after all.

I kneel down and place the wet kitchen roll against her

cut. She flinches from the coolness. I grimace apologetically. I wish I could take the pain from her.

'So, I'm waiting in the boardroom for this woman. Only Pickles will not settle, she's going fucking nuts, wanting to be not just sitting on me the whole time, but on my fucking neck. So, in a last-ditch attempt I took this bit of material I found on the table and I made a sort of baby sling for her. It was the only way to get her to calm the fuck down.'

I grin, imagining how stressed she must have been. She wrinkles her nose when she's stressed. It's kind of adorable. Adorable? What the hell am I thinking? I shake my head and go back to cleaning her leg as best I can.

'So, what happened?' I ask, leaning over to blow on it. Cool it down a bit.

Her shoulders slump in defeat. 'The executive came in for the meeting and... well, the product I was supposed to be photographing was the silk, very expensive scarf I'd tied around myself and this stupid fucking dog.'

'No!' I can't help but shout, barking out a laugh.

'Yes!' She snorts a sort of ironic laugh. Or maybe it's a cry. 'So, I had to hand it back to her, all covered in dog hair and dried mud.'

'Shit. Did she kick you out straightaway?'

'No.' She covers her face with her hands. 'She was all polite and insisted we carry on with the interview, but it was fucked the minute that happened. I was all flustered and couldn't get my words out. Then, just as we were leaving, Pickles decided to piss on their carpet.'

Oh my god. I rub at my eyes. What a bloody nightmare.

'Jesus.'

'Yeah. I had a few more choice words for her on the way home.'

I pick Pickles up. 'Why are you such a little nightmare?' She stares back at me, her big brown eyes pleading ignorance.

'Don't try to act innocent now,' she snaps. 'Look, we're gonna have to sort out some sort of doggy day care for her or something. I can't take her to work with me.'

Shit. How much is that going to cost? Another thing I didn't bank on.

'Yeah, you're right.' I nod. 'I'll look into it.'

'No, I will,' she insists. 'I'm not having her go to any old random.'

I smile back at her. Even when she's pissed her off this much she still loves her, deep down. Deep, *deep* down.

I notice a new framed photograph on the wall of Pickles. This soppy bitch is mad about her.

'I like the new photograph,' I say with a grin, nodding towards it.

She looks over at it. 'Thanks, but I'm not happy with it.'

She's such a bloody perfectionist.

I look at the time on my phone. 'I have to get back to work. Can I please leave her with you this afternoon and then we'll sort something?'

'Fine,' she sighs. 'What's another couple of hours of misery?'

I lift her chin, forcing her green eyes to look up at me. 'You promise you'd tell me if something else was bothering you?'

She stares back uncertainly, her mouth slack for a second, before she forces a smile.

'Promise.'

Why don't I bloody believe her?

Alice

I could have told him the truth. How I also got a text from my first ever boyfriend asking if the picture he attached was me. The porn revenge picture of me with everything out. I mean, what the hell was he thinking or trying to achieve? Make me feel like a pathetic slut? Check. Want to remind me how I'll never get away from it? Check again.

Either way he's managed to throw me into a slump. When Tom goes, I change into my pyjamas, take my make-up off and put on a rom com. The girls are always taking the piss out of me for my terrible taste in movies, but sometimes the crapper the better. You know what to expect, you get a happy ending and there's no drama you can't handle. Unlike bloody real life.

Pickles jumps up onto the sofa. I go to tell her off, but I don't have enough energy. She instead cuddles up on my lap. I stare down at her in shock. Can it be she senses I'm feeling low? I suppose she has to be good for something. It's definitely not walking.

Thursday 25th October

Alice

Today was Pickles' first day at her new doggy day care. She seems to have had a great time. She bloody should have for twenty quid! Not that I'm paying for it, thank God. Luckily, the dog carer agreed to be flexible with us. The days I'm not working I can look after her myself, even though she is a massive pain in the arse. I can't make Tom pay that out every day. He'd just be working to afford the dog care. Now I see why a lot of mums don't go back to work. It doesn't make sense.

Tom has been really sweet to me since my little breakdown yesterday. He even told me not to bother cooking and brought home a veggie pizza. I think it was just an excuse for him to have some BBQ chicken wings, but whatever. I scoffed it down, along with the Ben & Jerry's ice cream.

Once he picked Pickles up, he managed to talk me into going for a walk together along the sea front. Pickles does seem to be far better behaved with him. He bought her an extendable lead, so she can have some freedom, but we can still get her back.

Watching her now frolicking in the sea, it's hard to be pissed at her. She is kind of adorable.

Tom suddenly clasps my hand. I look down at our joined hands in shock.

'So how are you feeling today?' he asks casually, as if the guy isn't holding my hand. 'Better?' He gives my hand a quick squeeze and then let's go.

Wow. I can't believe how sweet he can be sometimes. It's weird and unsettling.

I force a smile I'm not feeling inside. 'Yeah, I'm feeling much better, thanks.'

He sighs and turns to look at me. 'Alice, look I know we're not besties or whatever. But if something is bothering you please know that you can tell me. Contrary to what people believe, I am actually a good listener.'

Pickles runs around us. 'I just...' Should I tell him about the naked pics? My crazy first boyfriend? No, no I can't. 'I just must be due on or something,' I quickly say.

His face squirms. 'Ew. Too much info, Ice Queen.'

I giggle. 'You said you wanted to listen,' I tease.

'Yeah, not to how your uterus lining is shredding thanks. Ugh, you women are gross. Anything that bleeds for seven days and doesn't die is a freak in my book.'

I burst out laughing. Then my leg is suddenly squeezed. I look down, ready to throw Tom's hand off when I realise it's Pickles' lead tightening around me. I try to look where I can untangle it but it's getting tighter by the second.

'Shit,' Tom gasps. 'She's wrapped us up.'

My body is suddenly smashed against Tom's, pressing my suddenly very erect nipples against his hard chest. Thank God for my coat hiding them.

'Pickles!' I shout.

Just at that second, I see her spot a seagull over the water. Her eyes widen. Oh no, please no.

She bolts across the water, the lead wrapping us so tight that we lose our footing and before we have a chance to correct ourselves we're falling into the freezing cold seawater.

It shocks me so much my mouth opens, taking in a mouthful of salty seawater. Tom manages to pull us up out of the water and drag us back to the pebbles. He lays me down and untangles us while shouting abuse at Pickles.

I'm so frozen I can't even speak. Every muscle in my body is frigid from the sudden change in temperature.

I'm finally free when he grabs Pickles and puts her on a tight lead. I take my soaking coat off my shoulders.

'You are never being allowed freedom again, missus!' he shouts at her. He turns to me, his eyes scanning over my tired body. 'Alice, you're gonna have to get up. We need to go. Now.'

'But I'm soaking wet. What's the rush?' Right now, I just want to lie here and feel sorry for myself a minute.

'Exactly,' he snaps bad-temperedly. 'Seeing you lying

there soaking wet with your nipples that could cut ice, has me sporting a raging boner. I'd like to get home before anyone notices.'

I look down at his bulging jeans and burst out laughing. 'Just when I thought you were being all sweet, you have to go caveman on me again.'

'What can I say, Ice Queen? You melted just enough to wake my dick up.'

Friday 26th October

Tom

I had to lock myself in my room and wank. It was the only way to get rid of my raging boner. But fuck me, seeing Alice laid there all wet... well, she's lucky I didn't jizz in my pants immediately. The woman's turning me into a teenager again.

I walk out into the kitchen.

'We're going to have to take the dog,' Alice says to me on a sigh. 'The dog woman can't have her.'

'Huh?'

'The Halloween party tomorrow night at the pub?'

'Oh yeah.' Jack did tell me the boys were coming down, so we were gonna make a night of it. 'It'll be fine.'

'Yeah, famous last words,' she snorts. 'Also, Tom, I think with you getting a boner today it'd be best if I slept in my own bed tonight. Alone.'

I can't help but feel my heart sink. 'Okay,' I shrug. 'Whatever. We were only doing it because of Pickles. I'm sure she'll be fine with just one of us.'

'Yep,' she nods. 'And if not, we'll just have to be strong.

It's not healthy for us to be sharing a bed. We're room-mates. Nothing more, right?'

'Right.' I nod. So then why do I feel like she just rejected me?

Chapter 14

Alice

After a fraught night of Pickles crying and pining for me, I managed to hold strong and not go into Tom's room. He must be knackered, but he also stayed true to his word and didn't bother me. The worst thing is that without his body heat I couldn't seem to sleep myself. It's funny how quickly you get used to sleeping with someone.

So that's how we find ourselves walking into O'Malley's with Pickles on a tight lead, our eyes heavy but our livers ready for a Halloween party battering. I've dressed Pickles up as a spider. She's wearing the cutest little antlers with fake spider eyes on top of her head.

I'm dressed as a circus ringmaster. It feels appropriate looking after this bunch of weirdos. Tom has come as Shaggy from Scooby-Doo on the promise that I'll let him dress Pickles as Scooby halfway through the night. I think he's going to use her to pull birds. Imbecile.

I've given Pickles a pep talk, so she knows to be on her best behaviour. Not that she seemed to take any of it in. God, if someone could just invent a machine which translates dog language it would make my life so much easier. Or is it sign language that is universal for every language? But then I suppose dogs don't have thumbs, do they? Bit hard for them. I giggle to myself.

'What are you thinking about?' Tom asks when we get to the bar. It's covered in fake cobwebs, gaudy plastic decorations, and candle filled pumpkins. 'You have the weirdest look on your face.'

I grin, feeling a flush light up my cheeks. 'Just... thinking about what I'm going to drink.' If I told him the truth, he'd think I'm even more of a freak than he already does.

'And?' he raises his eyebrows and with the green neon lights in the room he looks mischievous.

'I'll have a Southern Comfort and lemonade please.'

He raises his eyebrows disapprovingly. 'That's not very Halloweenie is it?'

I look heavenwards. 'Well, it's not actually Halloween tonight is it?'

He wrinkles his nose. 'Not with that attitude.'

The girls wave me over from their reserved booth with the guys. Thank God they're here. I feel like Tom has taken over my life. I need some girlie time. Though I doubt I'll get it tonight with two of the girls in question being loved up.

Erica and Jack have come dressed as Harley Quinn and Joker from Suicide Squad. About as scary as they could manage probably. Brooke and Nicholas are like a different couple entirely. Brooke has come as some kind of slutty jester with half her face painted and bloodied up. It's so good, it's obvious that Erica did it. Brooke always uses her make-up artist skills when she wants to look amazing.

Nicholas looks terrifying. He's dressed in his usual kind of clothes, but his face is completely painted white, with huge black lips, and his eyes drawn bigger around them. When he closes his mouth, he looks like demented clown. It might actually haunt my dreams.

Molly is dressed as a bloodied-up Barbie; of course she is. While Charlie is dressed as Deadpool, mask and all. That outfit is a bit too tight for him. If he wasn't my friend, I'd probably be taking the piss out of him.

Tom comes back a minute later with a tray full of shots, no Southern Comfort and lemonade in sight. Damn, that man never listens.

'Blood clot shots for everyone!' he shouts, like a woo girl. He's such a bimbo.

I tentatively take one of the red, gross-looking things. The top of it looks like burnt puss or something. 'What's in it?'

'Jack Daniels and cider with some burnt marshmallows on top.'

'And probably loads of food colouring,' Evelyn says holding it up to inspect it. She's dressed as Audrey Hepburn, which is basically how she dresses anyway. Trust her to not join in with the fun.

'Ah, so not that alcoholic then.' I take it and knock it back, the sugary sweetness sliding effortlessly down my throat and instantly warming my tummy. 'Mmm, it's nice. Can I have another?'

Tom's eyes widen. 'Wahey! Alice is on it tonight!'

Jack jerks his head towards Tom. 'None of that tonight,' he warns, his eyes serious.

What does he mean by that?

'Huh? None of what tonight?' Molly asks looking between the two of them.

'Nothing,' Tom says, rolling his eyes as if Jack is being ridiculous.

Within two hours I'm pretty drunk. Don't get me wrong, I can hold my liquor, but the way I've been chucking back these drinks I'm feeling nicely buzzed. Possibly too buzzed to be looking after a little dog. I've already dressed her up as Scooby-Doo to appease Tom and put a picture on Instagram. Poor cow.

I offer to get the round in and stand up on wobbly legs, giggling to myself. *Pull it together, Alice. You're a grown woman for God's sake.* I pass the lead over to Tom.

I pull my shoulders back and skip over to the bar. That's the only way to describe it. I find when I'm drunk I can't walk slowly, or I'll fall over. It's easier to do a sort of whimsical skip in my heels. Plus, I get to the bar quicker.

I order our drinks and look around the bar. That's when I notice the fitty sitting next to me is already looking at me with a devilish smile. Where the hell did he come from? I would have thought I'd have noticed this gorgeous hunk of meat walking in. He's all tall, dark, and handsome. Totally my type. Unlike Tom with his stupid blonde hair.

'Hey, gorgeous,' he says with a wink, and is that an Irish accent?

I giggle. I can't help it. Who on earth says 'hey gorgeous'? And the wink? Totally over the top. I'd eye roll in any normal situation, but this isn't a normal situation. It's Halloween and I'm feeling giddy after a few too many bloody themed cocktails. Plus, did I mention he's pretty?

'Hey yourself,' I say with what I hope is a seductive wink back. Knowing me he'll ask me if I'm okay in a minute. Think I'm having some sort of stroke.

'So, do you have any Irish in you?' he asks.

I stare back at him. It's too noisy in here. I can't concentrate.

'No,' I say with a headshake. 'Just here for a night out.'

'Do you want some?' he asks, throwing his head back on a chuckle.

Oh my god, the blatant cheek of him! Asking if I want a poke. Want to see the gold at the end of his rainbow, the cheeky fucker.

'You cheeky bastard!' I laugh, smacking him playfully on his shoulder. God, this guy is so not my type, but he's so audacious that I can't help but find him charming. And after the last couple of days I can't help but feel flattered.

He says something quietly, so quietly I can't hear him. 'What?'

'Come closer,' he says, guiding me towards him. It's only when I'm close to him that I notice instead he whips his head round and pecks a quick kiss on my lips.

I stare back at him in shock. Did he really just kiss me without my consent? Did I like it? What is happening right now?

I look down at his lips, licking my own. My eyes meet his, daring him to do it again. Who am I right now? Kissing a total stranger in a bar. I'm only ever this brave at Halloween. The freak in me comes out to play.

He lowers his lips, this time pressing them against me longer. His tongue teases at my mouth. I'm just about to allow him entry when I'm yanked back.

What the hell is happening?

I look around to see Tom's furious face, his eyebrows so furrowed he's going to give himself a permanent wrinkle.

He has my arm in his hand. 'What the hell, Alice?' he shouts over the music.

'Shit, is this your boyfriend?' the random kisser asks on a grimace.

'No!' I shout in disgust, throwing off Tom's hand. 'What the fuck is your problem, Tom?'

'I...' he puts his hands through his hair, his movements tense and jerky. 'I need to speak to you.'

'Yeah, well there are ways and means, buddy,' random kisser says on a huff.

Wow, he's a bit bloody mad considering I've just met him.

Tom's jaw turns to steel and I swear I can almost hear him growl. 'Mind your own fucking business,' he spits.

'That's what I was doing,' random Irish kisser says, 'when you butted head first like a bull into mine. We'd be kissing now *if it wasn't for you pesky kids,*' he jokes.

I burst out laughing. This guy is funny AND fit. Anyone who uses Scooby-Doo puns is a winner in my book.

'Alice is NOT your business,' Tom snarls, his eyes turning dark. I've never seen him so mad in my life.

Random kisser snorts. 'Sounds like you want her to be yours though.'

Oh no he didn't!

I turn to see Tom rear back his hand and punch him right on the jaw. Random kisser falls off his stool, clutching his face. What the fuck?

'Tom!' I shriek. Everyone is staring at us.

Nicholas, Charlie, and Jack are beside us within seconds.

'Get him out of here,' Jack instructs me, immediately taking control of the situation.

Why the hell is he my problem? I'm not his girlfriend.

I grab his arm and pull him towards the exit. I grab Pickles from Brooke, exchanging a quick eye roll, before taking him out of the pub, while everyone stares on, obviously enjoying the drama. Talk about ruin the night.

As soon as the fresh air hits us, the reality of what's just happened dawns on me. I kissed someone. Tom punched them. Why did that guy make him so angry?

'What the hell, Tom?' I demand, hand on my hip.

'I should be saying the same bloody thing to you!' he roars. 'What the hell are you doing kissing that random arsehole?' he howls back.

'I can kiss whoever the hell I want!' I yell, my finger pointed in his face. 'What has it got to do with you?'

'It's got everything to do with me!' he explodes, arms wide in the air.

I shake my head in disbelief. 'How does it have anything to do with you? We're roommates, remember?'

He stops pacing to stare at me. 'Is that all we are?' he challenges, his eyes full of something I can't put my finger on.

'Isn't it?' I ask, my voice low. Why don't I sound pissed off anymore? I'm still mad as hell, but... well, when he's looking at me with that sincerity and vulnerability in his eyes... I just, well, I don't know.

'If anyone is going to be kissing you, it's going to be me.'

I stare back into his emerald eyes. I'm waiting for him to break into laughter and tell me he's only joking. To call me a dickhead. Only he doesn't. He just continues to stare intently, not breaking eye contact with me for a second.

'You?' I whisper in disbelief.

He grabs me around the waist, pulling me into his chest. 'Me.'

He crushes his lips against mine, making me take a sharp inhale of breath through my nose. My eyes spring open in disbelief, looking back at his relaxed closed ones. I can't believe Tom is kissing me right now. What the hell is happening?

I force my eyes shut in a desperate bid to think. Think

of if I want this. Damn, this alcohol has my brain all fuzzy. Tom kisses me softly, each peck causing more goose-pimples to rise on my body. Oh, who am I kidding? His lips are smooth as velvet and he smells of woody sandalwood and cedar. I want him bad.

I let myself relax into it, his hand traveling up my neck and into my hair which he fists. It's almost rough, slightly painful, but I love it. He licks the seams of my lips, begging entry. I open my mouth willingly, letting his tongue come in to tease me.

He massages my tongue with his as his other hand leaves my waist to travel down to my arse. He squeezes an arse cheek hard, pulling me even closer into him. So close that I can feel his erection. Jesus!

This shit just got real.

I pull back, the feel of his dick against my stomach enough to wake me up. *What the hell are we doing? We're room-mates. This can't happen.*

'Tom,' I say feebly, my hand against his chest. His big strong, manly chest.

He looks back down at me, his chest heaving underneath my hand. I can feel his heart racing.

'What?' he asks, as if this is no big deal. To him it probably isn't. He probably gets off with women on a daily basis. That's the problem. I refuse to be part of his harem.

I force an unnatural laugh. 'We can't do this.'

He frowns. 'Why not?'

'Because we're roommates. It'll just make everything awkward.'

'So, you don't want this?' he challenges, eyebrows raised in disbelief. He's such a cocksure prick.

'I don't,' I say defiantly.

A white lie that might hurt him now but give him half an hour and he'll be over it. Onto the next girl.

He scoffs a sigh. 'Fine,' he snaps, standing further back from me. He looks down at the floor, then up straight into my eyes. 'Fuck you, Alice.'

He turns and walks away, his shoulders slumped.

Well that took a quick hideous turn.

I look down to see that in all the confusion I've dropped Pickles' lead, but she's still here, staring up at me faithfully.

Well, what the hell was that about? It's true what they say, anything can happen on Halloween.

Chapter 15

Sunday 28 October

Tom

I wake up in a bed that doesn't belong to me, my tongue stuck to the roof of my mouth. For a second, I think it might be Alice's, but as I look around and see the Flamingo bedspread, I realise I've not been that lucky. I turn to my left and spy the mass of blonde hair on the pillow. The duvet is pulled up around her face, so I can't make that out yet.

Shit. Who is this girl?

I try desperately to trace my mind back to last night. I left after Alice basically fucking gutted me, telling me she didn't want me, which I know is a fucking lie. You don't kiss someone back like that if you're not interested.

I went to another bar, had a few shots, and met some basic bitch at the bar. Ah, now I remember. Veronica. Or is it Verity? She had on a green bra and devil antlers and was all over me.

She offered me a few lines of coke in the toilet. God, why did I do it again? I'm such a dick. More shots. Some Jack Daniels and Coke. Then it goes blurry.

Jesus, I must have fucked her. Why the hell did I do that? Well, I obviously know why I did it. Because my dick rules my life. But said dick wants to be in Alice, not this woman.

She rejected me though. Told me she didn't want us to happen, even though her kiss said different. She thinks she's too good for me, and hey, maybe she's right. Doesn't stop it stinging though.

I'm pissed at myself that I wasn't strong enough to just go home. Instead I ended up being flattered by the first bitch to push her tits into my face and now I'm here. Alice will know I didn't come home last night. She'll jump to all sorts of conclusions that are probably true. Just proving to her I'm a no-good piece of shit that she should stay away from.

I check my watch. Eight am. Will Alice be awake already? God, with Pickles no doubt. She'll be pissed if she's had to go into the communal gardens to let her have a piss.

I creep slowly out of bed, careful not to wake blondie, and throw my clothes on. There's a used condom on the floor. Thank God, I was smart enough to wear one. I pick it up and throw it in the bin.

I walk out of the building and try to get my bearings. It doesn't help that I'm still new to the area. I look around and search for the sea. I spot it in the distance and head towards it. Once I get to the sea front, I'll be able to find my way home.

Forty minutes later, I put the key into the lock, fearful of her reaction. This is nuts. I'm acting like she's my mum. Or worse, a kind of wife figure. I have nothing to be embarrassed about. I'm just a single guy out doing his business.

As soon as I let myself in, I hear Pickles scurry around

the corner to meet me. At least I know someone's happy to see me. I pick her up and cuddle her into my neck. She's still got the most adorable puppy smell.

'Hey, girl, how are you?' I coo, looking into her big brown eyes.

I tentatively walk around the corner, ready to face the music. Deep breath, Tom. The only real person that can tell you off is your mum.

Alice is sitting on a kitchen chair in her jogging bottoms, a white vest with no bra, and her dressing gown over it. Fuck, I can almost see her nipples through it. She raises her eyebrows but doesn't say anything. She doesn't have to, it's all on her face.

'Yeah, yeah, where have I been? I stayed at a mates.' I quickly explain.

She rolls her eyes. She knows as well as anyone that all my mates were with her last night. God, I hate proving her point. Maybe I am a manwhore.

'None of my business,' she shrugs, taking another slurp of what I smell is coffee. God, I need one of those.

'You're right there,' I agree with a tight smile. I boil the kettle, trying to hide my simmering rage.

Who the fuck does she think she is being all judging? I put myself on the line last night and she shot me down. Well, some women want this. Are desperate for it in fact. I don't know why I've been waiting around for a frigid redhead when there's a whole sea of women I'm yet to bed. Brighton pussy here I come.

Monday 29th October

Alice

Tom didn't home again last night so I was stuck looking after his dumb dog. I've noticed that when I'm pissed at him I refer to Pickles as 'his' dog, not mine or ours. I know he will have spent the night with some skank, which to be honest makes me feel sick. He's so vile.

To think that our lips kissed and then he went straight to some whore—probably with my lipstick scent still on his lips—and kissed her. Ugh, it makes me crazy mad. Not crazy jealous you understand. Just, like angry that he's such a slag, and some girl is going to wake up and realise she was used by Tom 'Manwhore' Maddens. Poor bitch.

I'm still pissed at him. Not only to cockblock me, but then to kiss me. Where the hell did that come from? And with the whole *'if anyone is going to kiss you, it's going to be me.'* What the fuck? Someone has issues they need to look into. So basically, he doesn't want me, but he doesn't want anyone else to have me. Selfish, stupid bastard.

Not that I want him to want me. I wouldn't date that prick if he was the last man on earth. Just when I thought we might be turning into friends, he goes and pulls this.

He must have come home this morning while I was still sleeping to get dressed for work.

I hear the door creak open. I'm on the sofa with Pickles, eating Cheerios. I look like shit with scraped up hair, no make-up, and my jogging bottoms on. He drops his keys on the hallway table and scuttles in, looking far more ruffled than he did Friday night. Ironically, he looks more like Shaggy now.

'Hey,' he nods.

'Hi,' I nod back.

'I'm going to bed.'

And that's it. That's the apology I've been waiting for.

Wednesday 31st October

Alice

The last few days have been awkward, with an underlying tension. He's been getting home later and later each night, obviously in a bid to spend as little time with me as possible. At first I felt bad, having rejected him and all, but now I'm just pissed off. How dare he treat me like shit just because I told him no. Who the fuck does he think he is?

I've had a long week of taking shoe pictures in an attempt to network within the fashion industry. I'm just serving a vegetable curry to the table, unsure of when Tom's going to return when he comes skulking through the door.

'Hey,' I call, as he gets trampled on by Pickles. 'Good timing. I've just put dinner down.'

He comes around the corner, stroking the back of his neck. 'Ah, sorry. I've already eaten.'

He doesn't look sorry at all. In fact, he can barely look at me.

Fuck this.

I slam his bowl down onto the table. 'Did you not think to fucking text me to let me know?'

His eyes double in size. 'Jesus, chill out.'

'I've made too much now,' I complain, pointing to it as if it'll prove my point and somehow make him care.

He shrugs. 'Then you can just have it for lunch tomorrow.'

'The lentils will get soggy,' I shriek. Jesus, what has happened to me where I'm shrieking about soggy lentils?

'I'm sorry, okay,' he retorts like a grumpy teenager, 'but I needed some meat.'

Oh, now he's gonna throw this card at me. Make out I'm starving him. Bloody drama queen.

'Really?' I snarl. 'Because you don't sound sorry. In fact, you've been acting like a little bitch all week. Just because I rejected you doesn't mean you can treat me like crap. You have to respect my decision.'

His eyes meet mine and it's only then I see the hurt and vulnerability behind them. He looks like a lost little boy. You know, in a huge muscly body. Here I am assuming he's throwing his toys out of the pram when in actual fact I've hurt his feelings.

'I'm sorry,' he says, sighing wearily and running his hand through his hair. 'Things have been awkward, and I've been having a hard time at work. I'll try more from now on, okay?'

It's only then that it hits me; the reason I'm so mad. Because I've missed him. I've missed hanging out with him. Missed what has evolved into an easy kind of friendship.

'Okay,' I nod, glad he's conceding so easily. Brat boy Tom I can deal with. Hurt Tom not so much.

I start eating, just to have something to do. He sits down at the sofa and takes his shoes off with a groan. Jesus, he really is knackered. Anyone would think he was working in the mines with the way he's acting.

I desperately think of something to say to break the heavy silence. I know, the Peterborough trip.

'Me and the girls are going to Peterborough this Saturday, so if you want to jump in the car with us you can.' Actually, maybe he'd like me out of the way, so he can bring some tart back. 'Or just have the place to yourself here. Up to you.'

'Thanks. I'll think about it,' he nods. 'Why are you guys going? It's not Jack's weekend to see Esme.'

It's so cute that he knows their schedule. Little things like this warm my heart.

'Yeah, we know. Don't tell Jack or Erica, but we're going to try to reason with Amber about loosening up on Erica.'

'What?' he snaps, his jaw jutting out. 'Are you fucking mad? You girls are just going to make it all ten times worse.'

'No, we're not!' I snap back. God, he doesn't have much faith in me if that's what he thinks. 'We're just trying to cool down the situation. Make her see sense.'

'By ambushing her?' he scoffs, leaning back in the chair. 'How on earth does that sound like a good idea? I thought you were more practical than that, Alice.'

It hurts more than it should for him to be disappointed in me. Why do I care what a manwhore like him thinks?

'Hey! Look, it wasn't my idea, but I think it's a good one. Let her see we're not all monsters. We only want what's best for Esme.'

'Yeah, and you, a stranger to Esme, knows what's best for her.' I glare back at him. 'I just think it's a dickish idea. But who am I to tell you?'

I roll my eyes. 'Whatever. Look, if you care so much why don't you come with us? Make sure we don't ambush her as you're so scared of.'

He bites his lip as if mulling it over. 'I actually think that's a great idea. Plus, Esme hasn't met Pickles yet.'

I roll my eyes. 'Trust you to find the silver lining.'

But somewhere deep down I'm glad we'll be spending the weekend together.

Chapter 16

Tom

I can't believe I'm having to come along with Alice, Brooke, and Evelyn to see Amber. It's a shit show about to happen. How they think they'll be able to reason with Amber, I don't know. The girl is unreasonable at the best of times. How she's going to react with this trio in her face I have no idea.

The only thing I like about Amber is that she's a good mum to Esme, and it shows with how adorable and polite that little girl is. She's also never been a dick about Jack seeing her regularly. She's only being awkward now about Erica. Considering Esme is the most important thing in the world to her, I kind of get she'd be protective of who she spends time with.

But they've been together six months now. She needs to realise this is a permanent thing. With the way Jack talks about Erica, he sees himself marrying her and having more kids. Little half-brother and sisters for Esme.

I didn't think he'd ever settle down again after the bull-shit he went through with Amber, but then we didn't

127

expect him to bump into his first love on holiday in Luna Island.

It's weird being in such close proximity to Brooke who I've shagged, and Alice who I want to shag. Not that I do anymore. Nothing is more of a boner killer than being rejected. I definitely won't be putting myself out there again.

'We're here!' Evelyn sings as we pull into Amber's road.

She parks up and turns around to talk to everyone. Alice is next to me. I could feel her body heat pressing against me the whole way. Fucking torture.

'So, are we ready?'

'Ready,' Alice and Brooke nod.

'Let it be on record that I still think this is a bad idea,' I state, my muscles tense at the idea of this shit show.

Brooke rolls her eyes. 'Jesus, way to be a buzz kill,' she snaps. 'Charlie's Angels are about to sort some shit out.'

Charlie's angels? Charlie would love that shit.

I cross my arms over my chest. 'Or just create some more, but whatever.'

I open the door, take Pickles from Alice's lap and walk towards a grassy patch. She wees like she's been holding it in the whole time. Poor thing.

The girls get out of the car after me. As I watch from afar, I can't help but notice how they move like a unit, totally in sync with each other. Plus, those bitches are hot. Sometimes I forget, what with us all being together all the time. Sometimes it takes looking from afar to see them with fresh eyes again.

Alice tucks a strand of red hair behind her ear as they wait on Amber's doorstep. Something I've noticed she always does when she's nervous. I rush back over to them, so they don't get the door slammed in their face.

I push through them so I'm at the front. Amber

answers the door, smiling as she sees me and Pickles, but frowning when she takes in the others.

'What's going on?' she asks, her defences up quickly.

'We just want to talk to you,' Evelyn explains with a friendly smile. It's the friendliest smile I've ever seen come from her. Normally she's shooting daggers at me.

'Yeah, make you see sense,' Brooke says with a bitchy laugh. Well, she's not helping.

'We, erm,' I interrupt, 'wanted Esme to meet Pickles.' I present the cute puppy. 'That and have a cup of tea and a chat.'

She looks round at them warily. 'Okay, you can come in. But she can't.' She points at Brooke.

Brooke rolls her eyes, folding her arms over her chest, and in doing so pushes her breasts up to her chin. 'Fine, whatever. I'll walk to Nicholas' house. Call me after.'

The rest of us shuffle in, displaying polite smiles as she asks us how we want our tea. We go into the sitting room where Esme is playing with Barbie dolls. Her little eyes light up when she sees me.

'Uncle Tom!' she shouts, jumping up and running towards me.

That never gets old. I feel my heart explode. I crouch down to her, holding tightly onto a struggling Pickles. She obviously wants to jump all over Esme.

'Hey, baby girl.'

'And you brought your puppy!' she claps, jumping up and down. 'Daddy's been telling me about Pickles. She's so cute!'

'You okay if I let her down, babe?'

'Yes!' she squeals, clapping her hands together in glee.

I place her carefully down onto the carpet. 'Calmly, Pickles,' I warn. Like she'd listen even if she could understand me.

Pickles almost knocks her over, showering her in excitable kisses. Esme chuckles, only encouraging her.

The girls are behind me. 'Oh, and these are Erica's friends Alice and Evelyn.'

'They're pretty,' she smiles, playing with the edge of her dress. Something she always does when she meets new people.

Amber comes in with teas for everyone. So far so civilised.

'So,' Amber says when we're all settled. 'What did you come to say?'

Luckily, Esme's too preoccupied playing with Pickles to zone in on what we're saying.

Evelyn clears her throat. 'We're just here to tell you how amazing our friend Erica is and beg you to change your mind about letting Esme spend more time with her.'

Amber rolls her eyes. 'And this is your business because...'

'Because,' Alice joins in, 'she's our friend and Jack is her future. She wants Esme to be a part of that.'

'And what about me, huh?' Amber barks, her stare hard. 'I'm just supposed to roll over and let her take my daughter away from me?'

'That's not what she's trying to do,' Evelyn argues, her back straightening as if ready for a fight. 'Erica is one of the nicest people we know.'

'Yeah,' Alice nods. 'She knows she'd never take your place. And it's not like they're fighting for custody. They just want to be able to bring her down to Brighton occasionally. Let her enjoy the seaside.'

'So, she starts bugging me about moving there?' she snorts. 'I'm not stupid. I know their eventual plan. You've already got Jack and Tom living there. I won't be moving Esme.'

'That's not what they're asking,' I interject. Fucking women read too much into shit. 'They just want Erica to be involved in her life. I think you need to consider it. The way Jack's talking he's going to be marrying Erica eventually.'

I know from her reaction that it hurts to hear that. At one point she would have thought that she was getting the happy ever after with Jack. But she has to remember that they were a nightmare together. She was so jealous and possessive whenever he left the house.

We all wait for her to respond. Finally, she speaks.

'I'll think about it.'

'That's it?' Evelyn laughs. 'We travelled hours to come see you, and all we get is you'll think about it?'

Alice shoots her a dirty look. 'Evelyn!' She turns back to Amber. 'Sorry, she's just hungry. She gets really bitchy when she's hungry. Thanks for hearing us out.'

Amber nods but doesn't offer Evelyn a biscuit. I'm proud to see Alice has remained level-headed throughout the visit. The same can't be said for the other two.

'Right, Esme, we're going now, baby,' I announce with a smile. She jumps onto my lap for a cuddle. Having her little arms around me is the sweetest feeling in the world. I often wonder whether I'll ever have a child of my own. The thought of having a psycho mother does put me off though.

I squeeze her tightly, grab Pickles, and follow the girls out. Amber stops me before I make it into the hallway with the others.

'The redhead,' she smiles. 'Are you together?'

I feel my eyes bug out of my head. 'Huh? No!'

She laughs condescendingly. 'Okay, Tom. Whatever you say.'

Damn, how can that bitch read me? Is it that obvious? Am I putting out desperate vibes or something?

We leave and make our way over to the car.

'I should drop by my parents' while I'm here,' I announce, needing space from Alice. I need to get my head straight. Not that I bloody want to visit the 'rents. My dad is sure to give me a lecture.

'Well, I'm starving,' Evelyn says. I snort a laugh. She turns to glare at me. 'I'm heading straight for a pub lunch. Alice, you coming?'

She turns to look at me, a strange expression on her face. 'Actually, I'd quite like to meet the parents that created Tom 'Manwhore' Maddens.'

I feel my jaw hang open. She wants to meet my folks? That's kind of weird, but I nod instead, wondering what her angle is. Probably wants to slag me off to them.

Evelyn drops us off outside my house, apparently looking forward to face timing Fabio, or whatever her Luna Island boyfriend is called.

'You ready for this?' I ask Alice, taking a deep breath. 'My Dad can be...'

'What?' she asks with a frown.

I sigh and roll my eyes. 'He just thinks I'm not living up to my full potential.'

'Something we have in common then,' she snorts.

Great. They'll probably get on like a house on fire. Gang up on me.

I take out my key and let myself in. 'Mum, Dad,' I call. 'I'm back.'

'In here, love,' Mum shouts from the sitting room.

It's so nice to hear her voice again. I've been a bit of a shit and been dodging her calls, preferring to text her. The woman can talk for England and I'd rather not get stuck on the phone with her. But now, hearing her voice has me realising how much I've missed her.

We walk in to find her on a chair vacuuming above the curtain rail. Jesus, the woman's a liability.

'Hi, love,' she says, her eyes lighting up when she sees me. 'How's my little prince?'

Alice snorts behind me. 'Oh, and who is this lovely lady?'

I rush over to help her get down. 'This is Alice, Mum. My roommate.'

Her face brightens, and she stares at me in surprise. I suppose I never told her my new roommate was a bird.

'Well, it's lovely to meet your acquaintance,' she says, shaking her hand. God, I hate how she pretends she's posh when she meets new people. It's so embarrassing.

'Nice to meet you too,' Alice says, her eyes glinting at me with amusement.

Damn, I'm gonna hear about this later.

'And this must be Pickles!' She scoops down and takes Pickles from Alice. 'Oh, aren't you a dote!'

Pickles licks her face affectionately. That dog is such an attention whore.

'I had no idea you were coming home, or I'd have got some food in.'

Mama bear likes to keep me well fed. 'It's just a passing visit, Mum. We're headed back soon.'

Her face falls. 'Oh, I miss you so much, love. I've got that empty nest syndrome I think.'

I give her a quick cuddle. 'You know you can come down and visit me too, right? You'd love a weekend by the sea.' Oh shit. I probably should have checked with Alice first. 'I mean, if that's okay with you?' I add, with an apologetic grimace.

Alice smiles genuinely. 'Of course. We'd love to have you.'

The door bangs. Shit, Dad's home. The last time I saw him I was yelling that it'd be a while before I stepped back into this shit hole. Damn rebellious streak.

'Tom,' he says when he spots us, his eyes widening before he quickly pulls himself together. 'What are you doing here?'

'Good to see you too, Dad,' I say sarcastically.

'Of course, it is. Just surprised is all.' He looks at Alice. 'And who's your lady friend?' He looks her up and down disapprovingly, as he always would my women.

'This is Alice, my roommate.'

His face softens immediately. 'Ah, Alice. So lovely to meet you.' He shakes her hand. 'Thanks so much for taking our boy in on such short notice. Goodness knows he's not the most organised. If it weren't for you, he'd probably still be sleeping on Jack's sofa.'

'Oh, it's fine,' Alice says. 'He's actually a great room-mate. Very responsible.'

I stare back at her. She's lying for me?

'And this is Tom's new puppy, Pickles,' Mum says, presenting her like she's a trophy.

Dad stares down at her horrified. 'Tom, you got a dog? Why on earth would you think you're responsible enough for a dog? You're not even in stable accommodation yet.'

'My flat is very stable,' Alice says, as if hurt.

'What I mean is that it's not his flat. He only needs to annoy you enough and you'll be kicking him out on his ear.'

'Jeez, thanks, Dad.'

I look at my watch. We've been here less than seven minutes and I already need to leave.

'Anyway, we really need to get going. It's just a flying visit.'

Mum's face falls. 'Oh. Well, you know I'd love to see you more.'

I nod. 'I know, Mum. I'm just busy with work and stuff.'

'You should never be too busy to visit your mother,' Dad says, as if baiting me for an argument.

I ball my hands into fists. 'Yeah, well, maybe if you weren't riding my balls every time I did, I'd stop by more often.'

'Don't use that kind of language around your mother,' he snaps, his cheeks reddening.

I roll my eyes. 'Whatever. Mum, I love you, but I'm out of here.' I grab Pickles and hightail it out of there.

I keep walking until I'm at the green where me and the boys used to play when we were younger. I let Pickles down onto the lead. Alice's hand appears on my shoulder. I turn and look down at her.

She smiles sadly. 'I'm sorry.'

'For what?' I ask with a shrug, trying not to look bothered. I don't want her to think I'm some pussy.

'For your dad being on your case. I had no idea you weren't close.'

I sigh, not wanting to talk about it, but knowing she won't quit until I do. 'We were. He just thinks I can do better. Hated how I treated the place like a hotel.'

She smiles cheekily. 'I can imagine.'

I smile back, glad she's lightening the mood. 'But it seems even when I move out he's still nit-picking at my life.'

Her eyes soften. 'Don't let him get you down. You're doing great.'

I turn my body towards her fully. 'Am I really, Alice? If I'm such a catch, how come you rejected me?'

Shit, where did that come from?

Her eyes widen. 'I... I...'

It's my dad getting in my head and fucking everything up. 'Yeah, I'm a manwhore and you're too good for me. Got it.'

She balks, physically stepping back. 'Tom, that's not it.'

I scoff a laugh. 'Alright, Alice. Real convincing. Just forget it, okay? I'll get the train home tomorrow.'

With that, I turn and head towards Charlie's house. I need my boy right now. That and a bottle full of Jack Daniels.

Chapter 11

Monday 5th November

Alice

I can't believe Tom left me like that. The whole day was a bit of a head-fuck. First trying to keep everything calm between the girls and Amber, then meeting Tom's parents, and him having a go at me. Way to make everything awkward Tom.

I had no idea that Tom had taken my rejection so hard. I assumed for a manwhore like him, his ego would be battered for a few days and then he'd get over it. Move on to the next vagina with legs.

But there he was showing me he cared. Whether he cared about me, or just the fact that someone said no I'm still not sure. It can't have helped that his dad was so on his case. I was stunned he was so blunt with me there. My parents wouldn't dare be so rude in front of a guest. They're all about show and how things would look to outsiders.

I tried calling him when we were driving back, but he dodged my calls. He only got back late last night and went straight to bed. I despise this awkwardness. This is why

137

living with girls is easier, even Princess Barbie was a breeze compared to this.

So today I've decided I'm going to his work with a picnic. I don't care if he says he doesn't have time for lunch. I'll unpack it at his desk if I have to. This way we can discuss everything and get it out in the open. Pickles is at doggy day care, so we'll have no distractions.

I tell the woman at reception that I'm Tom's roommate and she buzzes me straight through. God, I could be any nutter. I go into the open plan office searching for him as people stop, turn, and stare at me. Yes, I suppose I could have done with a more low-key outfit, but what can I say? I dress to impress.

I'm wearing my turquoise floral tea dress, and my red, satin, polka-dot peep-toe heels, with my navy cape keeping me warm. I knew if I wanted to win back Tom's affections I'd have to look the part. Men are always so visual, and I'd guess Tom is even more so. He can't resist a pretty girl, especially one with food.

I'm just about to give up when a young guy walks up to me. 'Hi, can I help you?' He can't stop looking at my shoes. Pervert.

'Yeah, I'm looking for Tom Maddens.'

He smiles. 'Well, Tom's a lucky man. He's just around the corner to the right.'

'Thanks.' I force a polite smile and move on quickly. Creep.

I'm just rounding the corner when I spot him at the printer. I'm just about to call out to him when a woman in her forties or fifties with far too much make-up on sidles past him, pauses and strokes his bum. Did I really just see that right?

Tom jumps out of his skin, then turns to face her, his skin pale. He smiles, but even from here I can tell it's forced. His eyes aren't wrinkled, and I can tell he's uncomfortable by how he's standing. She winks at him and walks away. What the hell was that?

He turns fully around and spots me, his face lighting up with a genuine smile. I can't help but feel special.

'Alice,' he says walking towards me. 'Hey. Is everything okay?'

'Yep, all fine. I'm just here to take you out for lunch.' I raise the basket as if to prove it.

'Oh. Okay, let me just grab my phone.'

He darts towards his desk, grabs it and then walks back over.

'That looks heavy. Want me to carry it?'

Sometimes it's hard to digest when he's being such a gentleman. It's easy to forget he has manners when half the time he's acting like a prepubescent little boy.

'I even made you a ham sandwich.'

His mouth gapes open just as we go outside. 'You're joking? You bought and touched meat?'

I stifle a giggle. 'Okay, no. I bought it at the deli already done.'

He shrugs with a laugh. 'You still paid for it.'

'Yep,' I nod. 'You owe me three-pounds-fifty.' He turns to look at me, eyes wide. I burst out laughing.

'Yeah, you're bumped,' he grins. 'I'm going to call your veggie leader and report you.'

I roll my eyes. 'We're not a cult, Tom. We just don't like eating flesh.'

He raises his eyebrows. 'No need to be so dramatic. Anyway, where do you wanna eat?'

'What about this park?' I say, pointing across the road. 'Perfect.'

He shocks me by looping his arm through mine. I look down at it then back at his face. It's as if he hasn't even noticed the unconscious action, instead concentrating on crossing us over the road safely.

As soon as we've crossed and are onto the grass, I bend over and take my shoes off. I don't want to get them ruined and I love any chance to get my feet onto grass or sand. To really feel the earth underneath my feet. It's quite fair today, with only a slight chill in the air.

I take the blanket from my basket, lay it down next to some pretty violas, and perch on the edge. Tom flops down onto his stomach next to me.

'Give me the ham sandwich.' he says, his eyes lit up with excitement.

I hand it over and then get out my feta salad. 'So, who was that cougar that grazed your arse earlier?'

He frowns, looking down at his sandwich. 'Huh?' he asks, vaguely. It's clear he doesn't want to elaborate.

Tom acting shy and vague? This must be a bigger issue than I first thought.

'You know exactly who I'm talking about. Who is she?'

His shoulders slump. 'She's my boss.'

I freeze with my fork mid-air. 'Are you fucking kidding me?'

His boss is touching his arse? How fucking inappropriate is that? I thought it was bad enough when it was some horny colleague, but his boss? That's bloody sexual harassment in the workplace.

'Nope. My boss.'

Then it dawns on me. He's sleeping with his boss, or at least has slept with her in the past. Probably regrets it now that she's wanting more.

'You're sleeping with her?' I blurt out.

His eyes nearly pop out of their sockets, then sadden. 'Really, Alice? That's the first thing you think? That I'm sleeping with her?'

Ooops. But... yeah, of course I thought he was sleeping with her.

'I'm sorry. So... you're not?'

He rolls his eyes. 'No, Alice. Jesus, is that so hard to believe? But she wants me to. It's getting awkward as fuck.'

'Shit, Tom, you need to report her. She can't get away with that.'

He rolls his eyes. 'Well, she is.'

How can he be so laid back about this? If this was happening to me he'd be the first one to kick off. Probably try to kill the guy.

'Wait, how long has this been going on?' I ask, staring at him intently.

He tries to shift his eyes away from me, but I follow them and wait until he's staring back. He blows out a breath in a clear attempt to relax himself.

'Since I started,' he finally admits. 'But it's fine, she's just a woman.'

I nearly choke on my salad. 'Okay, first of all, no one is *just* a woman. And secondly it doesn't matter what sex she is. It's sexual harassment.'

He scoffs a laugh. 'I'm a big boy. I'm not gonna get talked into sleeping with her.'

'That's beside the point!' I bark, nearly losing it. 'She shouldn't be doing this at all. If it were a man doing this to a new female employee, you'd think it was outrageous.'

'Yeah, but I'm not some meek female. Seriously, I can handle it.'

Meek female? This man is such a cave boy.

I roll my eyes heavenwards. 'Ugh, fine.' I throw myself down onto the grass and look up at the sky. A big grey cloud is looming, threatening to cover our sunshine soon. It reminds me of our current situation and why I'm trying to offer an olive branch.

I roll onto my side.

'Anyway, Tom. I wanted to talk about us.'

He frowns. 'There is no us.'

Ouch. I get up and walk over to the violas, attempting to cheer myself up. That's why I like them, they always seem so happy with their smiley look.

'Look, you seem to have taken my rejection really hard. I just wanted to say that it's not that I don't like you.'

'You just don't fancy me?' he asks with a cocky smile.

I think about it for a second, pretending to study the violas. 'No, I do fancy you.' His mouth falls open. 'In fact, sometimes when I'm around you, I feel myself starting to act like an idiot and that's why we can never be. I need to focus on my career right now, and I can't let any silly infatuation take up my time.'

He grins, his eyes devilish. 'Infatuation? Alice, are you infatuated with me?'

I sit back down and snort a laugh. 'No. I didn't mean it like that.'

He shuffles closer, our faces so close I can feel his breath against my cheek. He trails his thumb down my cheek, causing goose-pimples in its wake. I try with all of my might not to lean into his hand when in reality I want nothing more.

I close my eyes in a bid to escape his searching stare. When I open them he's still there, still looking at me in wonder as if I'm the most perfect thing he's ever seen. I stare down at his lips. God, I could just move a few centimetres and they'd be on mine.

I bite my lip subconsciously.

'You're killing me here, Alice.' Tom whispers, his voice husky.

I'm just about to lean in when a big fat droplet of water hits my nose. I look up in bewilderment. The dark cloud is over us now. Another rain droplet falls before a heavy shower takes hold in seconds.

'Shit!'

We both jump up, throw the food into the basket and Tom grabs it. Using the blanket to shelter us, we run to stand under a huge oak tree people have congregated under. We shiver, attempting to shake off some of the rain from our bodies.

I can barely look Tom in the face. I can't believe I was going to kiss him! What is going on with me?

'I'm sorry your dad was a dick to you,' I blurt out over the thundering shower, desperate to change the subject away from us.

He politely smiles with a nod, his gaze falling to the floor. 'It's fine. He's not always been like this. I think I've just pushed him too far over the last few years.'

I chuckle. 'And I bet it doesn't help that your mum thinks the sun shines out of your arse.'

He laughs. 'I can't help it if I'm her little prince.'

My God, no wonder he's so self-assured and useless around the house. That mother has spoilt him rotten.

'Anyway, your dad wasn't even that bad. If you met my parents, you'd have a bloody shock.'

This seems to pique his interest. 'Why are they so bad?'

I shrug. 'They're not, I suppose. Just... very judgemental and standoffish.'

'No way?' he laughs. 'I saw you being raised by hippies.'

'What? Because of the red hair and wacky clothes? God, Tom, you're so one-dimensional.'

'Hey! No, I'm not.'

'Whatever. I actually felt more welcome at your parents than I ever have at mine.'

'You're having me on. They can't be that bad!'

I scoff. 'Trust me, I'm not. I have to go for dinner this weekend for my mum's birthday and I'm already dreading it.'

'I'm gonna have to see this to believe it, I'm afraid,' he challenges, his arms crossed over his chest.

'What?' I splutter. 'You want to come to Sunday lunch with my family?'

He nods.

'You're insane! Why on earth would you want to put yourself through that?'

'Because I think you're being dramatic, and because I want to see what kind of people created Alice.'

I can't help but feel flattered that he wants to know more about me. Not that I'm anything like those people.

'I am not a representation of these people. I'm this awesome *despite* coming from them.'

He frowns for a second. 'Wait, are you saying they like...' he drops his voice to a whisper, 'abused you or something?'

'God, no! They're not that bad. They're just stuck up is all.'

'Well then, fine. Tell them to fix one extra place setting. I'll be there.'

Wednesday 7th November

Tom

I meet Jack at the gym after work. I need to work away some of this tension in my body. Between the flirtatious boss whose attention I don't want, and Alice's wavering attention that I'm desperate for, I'm a big ball of stress.

Plus, it doesn't help that Alice's bedroom is only across the hallway from mine. Whenever I wank, I'm terrified she's going to hear me and know I'm doing it.

I'm already on the treadmill when Jack joins me on the next one, fuming. I've known him long enough to know by his red ears and tense jaw.

'Who shit in your milkshake?' I ask him with a grin.

'It's not funny,' he snaps. 'I've just got off the phone with Amber. She says the girls went down at the weekend and confronted her about her issues with Erica.'

'Oh.' Shit. She grassed on us. Wait, it doesn't sound like she said I was there, so I'm in the clear for now. 'What was she saying?'

'Ugh, she was screaming that any decision she makes will be hers and she won't be intimidated by Erica's mates. Can you fucking believe they were stupid enough to do that? They've made everything one hundred times worse.'

Shit. I have to tell him.

'Look, they were only trying to help.'

He turns to stare at me, almost falling off the treadmill. 'You mean, you assume they were trying to help?'

I look down at my feet.

'Right, Tom?' His voice is rising more by the second. 'You didn't know about this, did you?'

I blow out a defeated breath. 'Okay, I did.'

'Are you fucking kidding me? How could you not have warned me?'

A few people turn to stare at us.

'Look, I tried to talk them out of it,' I say quietly, waiting for the spectators to get bored and look away. 'But you know that lot when they get an idea in their head. They're unstoppable. So...'

'So...?' Jack asks, his jaw ticking with rage.

'So, I kind of went with them.'

'WHAT?' More people turn to stare.

'Only to make sure they were restrained! And Jack, they were. I kept everything calm. If she's saying they were rowdy, she's talking crap.'

He slows down the treadmill until it stops. 'She said if I ever want Esme down here then I'll have to take her to court.'

Shit. I can't believe Amber is being so bloody unreasonable. I mean, I get that she's her mother and is going to be protective, but Jack has always been a stand-up father. I don't think he's asking for much. He's said he'd drive up there to collect her and it wouldn't be every time he had her.

'Maybe it's time to think about court then?'

He sighs. 'But how much will that cost? It's not like I have shit loads in savings.'

'Just speak to a solicitor. Get an idea. You'll feel better after.'

'Okay. You're right.' He slaps me on the back. 'Thanks, Tom. I'm so glad I've got at least one of you that lives here now. Even if you do insist on doing stupid shit behind my back.'

I roll my eyes. 'Don't be getting emotional on me, Jack. I'll have to go and buy you tampons.'

Chapter 18

Alice

The gang decided to go out tonight for fish and chips seeing as we didn't get to spend fireworks weekend all together. We've just settled down on the pebbled beach with food when the girls zone in on me.

'So, are you and Tom together now or what?' Evelyn asks me, always right to the point.

I roll my eyes. 'No. I keep telling you guys.'

'Oh please,' Brooke says with an eye roll. 'You guys are so into each other.'

'No, we're not,' I say quickly. 'I turned him down, remember?' I whisper so the boys won't hear us.

'Whatever,' Erica snorts. 'At least this one lives in the same country,' she says pointedly at Evelyn. Evelyn huffs. She turns back to me. 'Why are you running away from it? You know he likes you.'

I sigh. 'Maybe because I have the worst taste ever in men and Tom could be top of that list. A male chauvinist, sexist pig with commitment issues. Ooh, yeah, sounds like a right catch.'

'Tom's not like that,' Molly says, as if I've hurt her feelings.

'You barely know him, Moll! And you always see the best side of everyone anyway.'

She shrugs. 'I don't see how that's a bad thing.'

I touch her on the shoulder. 'It's not. But I have to be more practical. The last boyfriend put bloody revenge porn up! It's clear I'm not a good judge of character.'

'So, you do like him then?' Brooke asks with raised eyebrows, an amused smile playing on her lips.

'I obviously like him. As a friend. As a roommate. And do I fancy him? Yeah, I probably do, but that doesn't mean I should let my vagina do my thinking for me.'

'Really?' Brooke chuckles. 'You should try it sometime.'

'We can't all be you, Brooke,' Evelyn says with a disapproving tut.

Nicholas calls her over. 'So true.' She stands up. 'See ya.'

'I agree with you anyway,' Evelyn says to me, still serious. 'You're just being sensible.'

It's because she hates Tom and thinks he's a giant pig. I don't blame her, I thought the same not so long ago. I kind of still do in a way.

'Well I don't,' Erica argues. 'I say follow your heart.'

That girl watches too much Disney.

I look over at Tom laughing away with Charlie. My heart doesn't feel full whenever I look at him, it feels pained. Afraid. I'm living in fear that one more heartbreak will shatter me forever.

I take out my vintage camera I bought at a car boot sale for a frigging steal. The poor bastards didn't realise I'd robbed them. I start taking a few natural shots of the group and then Pickles against the pebbles.

Tom walks over with Brooke. 'You guys fancy coming back to ours for a movie?' he asks everyone.

'I'm up for that,' Brooke nods. 'As long as we can have a walk through the lanes first. I still haven't got Nic a birthday present.'

'Brooke! It's on Wednesday!'

'I know,' Brooke laughs. 'Hence the wanting to walk through the shops.'

We agree, and I pretend to insist to the lads that I want to have a little shop on the way back. They all groan but Brooke smiles back appreciatory.

'Tom, you're going to have to be our lookout, so Nicholas doesn't cotton onto what Brooke's doing.'

He rolls his eyes but agrees.

He looks down at my camera. 'Why are you using that old thing? Isn't digital easier?'

I nod. 'Yes of course it's easier, but oh my god, I just love the finish with old cameras. I mean, it is a pain in the arse having to get them printed properly. In an ideal world I'd have my own dark room, but I haven't won the lottery yet.'

Brooke stops to look in a shop with old musical instruments. Just then I notice my favourite antique jewellery shop up ahead.

'I'm just going to have a look here,' I shout to the others.

I look in at the lit-up display. It's like a treasure chest of precious jewels. I will never understand how people want normal store-bought jewellery. Stuff that everyone else has. Mass-produced, factory made stuff. I much prefer one-off pieces like this, with a story, with a life they were a part of before they came to be in my possession.

A gorgeous brooch catches my eye. It's gold with

gemstones in it. I notice that they're the birth stones for me and the girls. That's a weird coincidence.

'What are you looking at?' Tom asks, jogging up behind me.

'Oh nothing,' I say turning and walking back towards Brooke. I really need to help her with a present for Nicholas. Not looking at jewellery I can't afford.

After a painful hour of shopping we finally help Brooke buy Nicholas an antique lighter which we hope he'll love. The truth is that the guy is impossible to shop for. I've just got him a vintage t-shirt I saw in a shop a few weeks back. It made me think of him.

We bring everyone back to our flat after for drinks and put on a scary film with a particularly bad actress with huge breasts that the guys joke about. Erica and Jack fall asleep almost immediately. I have no idea how when there are women screaming on-screen, but they manage it. I suppose we did turn all the lights off to freak ourselves out.

It's coming to a particularly tense bit when I feel someone tap me on my left shoulder. I turn around quickly, knowing no-one is to that side. There's no one there. What the hell?

I look around and find Tom smirking next to me, on my right-hand side.

'Was that you?' I ask, sure he wouldn't be so juvenile.

'No!' he says, mock offended.

'You're such a dick,' I can't help but chuckle. 'Why would you do that in the middle of a horror film?'

'Because I'm bored,' he says with a boyish smile. The light of the television reflects on his amazing green eyes, lighting them up.

'Pick on someone else,' I say jokingly.

'Look around you,' he says with a wave of his hand. 'There is no one else.'

He's right. Brooke and Nicholas are making out in the corner, Evelyn's dozed off, and Molly and Charlie are playing rock, paper, scissors.

'Are you not watching the film?' I whisper.

'This shit can't scare me,' he scoffs, puffing out his chest like Tarzan.

We go back to watching the screen, but now I'm super aware of how close to me he is. I can't help glancing over to his face, trying desperately to be as discreet as possible. He really has got the most perfect skin. There's not one blemish on it. He's clearly never known the struggle of pimpled skin.

The music on screen turns tense. Oh god. Something jumpy is about to happen. I force myself to watch it. Oh god, creepy killer guy is going to jump out any minute. I can feel it.

I wait another agonising thirty seconds before the killer jumps out from behind the washing machine. Fuck! How did he even get behind there?

Tom and I both jump out of our skins. I look down to see that I've got my hand on Tom's thigh. I look up into his face. His lips are parted as he pants from the surprise. The light of the TV is the only thing reflecting onto his face making him look like some sort of ethereal God. I definitely shouldn't have drunk that wine.

In that moment I want nothing more than to lean in and kiss him. To be held in his arms and pretend—if only for tonight—that it wouldn't complicate things.

He licks his lips, not taking his eyes off mine. He leans in, only a mere millimetre, but enough for me to know he's going in for a kiss. Fuck it. I'm doing it. I'm going to kiss Tom.

I lean in slowly, so slowly he seems nervous that I'm going to change my mind. My lips are so close to his that I can feel his laboured breath on mine. Just closing the distance now. One more movement and I'll get to feel those plump lips on mine.

I close my eyes and I'm just about to close that tiny distance when Pickles barks loudly from across the room, making us both jump. We look over to her. She's standing by the door. She obviously needs a wee.

I look to Tom, embarrassed.

'Well, that's one way to ruin a moment, Pickles,' I say with a chortle.

We grin at each other like idiots. Tom stands. 'Until next time.'

And for once I really know what I want. I want next time to come quickly. No matter how much it fucks things up.

Saturday 10th November

Tom

Today we're all travelling up to Peterborough to take Esme to her school's Christmas fair. A bit early in my book, but apparently, they always do it around now to make way for Christmas parties and nativity plays in December.

Amber can't bitch because we're not leaving the area and she can't make it anyway. I'm in Jack's car with Erica, Evelyn, and Charlie. I deliberately made sure I was in a separate car to Alice. I need some space away from her to think.

We almost kissed last night. Hell, if we had, I'd have slept with her. I have a feeling that once I start with her it'll take an awful lot of willpower to stop. Her having that kind of power over me worries me. What is it with this girl? She's not even my type. Weird, tattoos, piercings, small tits. She's the opposite of my type.

What might have started as a bit of fun winding her up, has turned into something more. But I don't want a relationship, especially when I've just spread my wings from my mum and dad's house. I also don't want to hurt her. I get the feeling she's been fucked around by past boyfriends.

'So,' Charlie says when we're on the motorway, 'I caught you and Alice almost kissing last night.'

Erica's head swings round from the front. 'WHAT?'

Oh, for fuck's sake, why did he have to ask me here?

'You have to tell me EVERYTHING!' she demands, clapping her hands together. She's probably already planning our joint wedding.

'Shit, chill out, Erica. Nothing's going on.'

Jack scoffs a laugh. 'Yeah, right,' he says under his breath, but loud enough for us all to hear.

'Come on,' Charlie encourages, digging me in the ribs. 'We're all friends here.'

I look up to see Evelyn glaring at me. 'Don't put me on that list,' she says.

God, why does this chick hate me so much? You'd think she'd be happy now that she's in a relationship of her own. But no, this chick is constantly PMSing.

'Evelyn,' Erica snaps. 'Leave Tom alone. You wouldn't stand in the way of true love, right?'

She snorts. 'Don't give me all of that Disney crap. This is Tom 'Manwhore' Maddens here. He just wants to take what he needs from her and then throw her away.'

I curl my lip up in distaste. 'Fuck, Evelyn. What the hell did I ever do to you?'

'Me? Nothing. I'm too smart for you. I thought Alice

was too, but even she seems to be falling under your spell. I have no idea why.'

'What if I actually like her?'

She rolls her eyes. 'Guys like you aren't capable of actually liking women. You just want to club them around the head, drag them back to your cave and then be done with them.'

I frown. 'Wait, are you trying to call me a caveman?'

'Duh!' she snaps. 'Want me to spell it out for you? You're no good for Alice. Stay away from her.'

'Evelyn!' Erica shouts. 'Leave Tom alone!'

'Yeah,' Charlie says nodding in agreement. 'Tom's a good bloke.'

'Okay, name his last serious relationship?' she challenges with a quirked eyebrow.

Jack coughs. 'She's got you there.'

'Look, whatever me and Alice do is none of any of your business,' I roar. I've never wanted to punch a woman, but Evelyn pushes me. Maybe because I know half of what she's saying is the truth.

'Unless we have to pick up the pieces,' Erica warns with a kind smile. 'Admit it, Tom. How awkward would it be if you got together, ended things badly, and then we all still have to see each other all the time?'

'Yeah,' I nod begrudgingly. It's not like I haven't thought of that.

'She's been through enough,' Evelyn says absent-mindedly.

Through enough? What the hell does she mean by that? A bad ex-boyfriend like I thought?

Erica glares at her. 'Shut up, Evelyn.'

'Why? What's she been through?' I ask, looking between the two of them, desperately trying to read them. They're definitely communicating without talking here.

'Nothing,' she finally says, crossing her arms over her chest and looking out of the window.

'Just really think about it,' Charlie says with a slap on my back.

'Ok,' I promise. 'I will.'

It's all I can think about anyway.

Chapter 19

Alice

The car ride down felt even longer than normal. I still have no idea why Tom insisted on getting in Jack's car, when Molly was about to go in it. It's like he's avoiding me since last night. Did I read it all wrong? Did I maybe lean in and imagine he was into me at all? Maybe he was just being polite.

He's supposed to be coming with me to my parents' house tomorrow. That's probably off now. Just what I bloody need. My parents completely unfiltered.

Oh well. I've asked for a large glass of rosé to loosen me up a bit. I don't want to be terrified of being left alone with him. But apparently all they serve at this stupid school Christmas fair is mulled wine. I'll have to work with that then.

'Alright?' I look up, following the voice, to find Tom holding out a mug of the stuff. Damn it.

'Thanks,' I nod, hurriedly taking it off him. I take a large gulp. It's so hot it burns my tongue, but I try not to react. I don't want to look like a raving idiot.

I keep my eyes on the floor, willing for him to go away. The others are around us, but I could really do with him just fucking off somewhere else. Instead I feel him sit down beside me on the bench. Ugh, I hate all this awkwardness.

I'm just about to say something to break the unbearable silence, when Esme comes running, throwing herself into Tom's arms.

'Uncle Tom!' she shouts in glee.

He throws her easily into the air, catching her just as easy. 'Hey, short stuff. You ready to find some Christmas chocolate?'

'Yeah,' she giggles while he tickles her. 'I bet I'll find more than you.'

He grins back at her. 'Is that right?'

'Yep,' she nods, beaming back at him. 'Daddy says you're rubbish at finding things.'

'Did he really?' he laughs. 'Come on then. Let's go find that chocolate.'

I sigh as I watch them, along with the other guys, going along the stalls of festive chocolate and homemade presents. They're all so goofy with her. Fighting over themselves to buy her things. It has her in hysterical giggles most of the time.

'Aren't they adorable?' Molly asks, suddenly sitting down beside me.

I nod. 'Mmm.'

'I know you like him, you know?'

I huff out a breath. 'God, I am so sick of being told what I feel. Do you know how frustrating that is?'

'Sorry, but it's true.'

'Do you know what's true, Molly?' I snap. 'The truth is you like Charlie.' Her mouth drops open. 'You really like him, and you don't know what the fuck to do with that information.'

'What... what are you talking about? What do you mean?' Her nose starts turning red.

'I mean that you're letting the fact he has a penis stand in the way of your happiness.'

Her eyes dart from left to right. 'I mean... I like him as a friend, but you know I'm gay.'

'All I'm saying is that I see how you look at him when he's making you laugh. You've had the same look on your face when you've looked into old girlfriends' eyes.'

She shakes her head. 'You're wrong.'

'Whatever. Unlike you, I don't force my opinion on others. Do whatever you want, but just let me get on with my life.'

I feel terrible as soon as I storm away. I mean, yes, I've been thinking it a while, but that doesn't give me the right to sound off to Molly. That girl has never hurt a fly.

I go into the women's toilets for a breather, but really, it's made for little girls, with tiny sinks and miniature toilets. I neck my mulled wine. I decide I'm going to go straight to the mulled wine stall once I've pulled myself together. Get another large mug. Fuck it, I might get two.

This is why I hate getting involved with men. They bring nothing but anxiety. I take a deep breath and try to focus my thoughts. Not let them wander into how awkward it's going to be when we're at home. I try to focus myself. What can I see? I can see the toilet roll holder. The small sink in the corner. What can I smell? Ugh, yucky disinfectant. Well at least it's clean.

I count to ten. Then again but backwards. My heart rate has started to go back to semi normal. I can do this. Just one more mug of wine and I'll be close to not caring. I can just sleep on the way back in the car.

I take one more deep breath before opening the door and bolting out—straight into a wall. At least that's what it feels like. I look up to see Tom staring down at me. I place my hand on his chest to push myself off him, but the heat underneath my hand makes me pause.

I look back up at him into his gorgeous face. His strong jaw.

'Are you okay?' he asks, his voice low with a husk to it.

I blink up at him, in a daze. He's just so goddamn pretty.

'The guys said you looked upset. You okay?'

I exhale out a big breath.

'Yeah. I just... I'm just tired, is all.'

He smiles weakly. 'Come here.'

He wraps his arms around me and pulls me closely into his chest. I think about fighting it, but I wasn't lying. I am tired. Tired of caring. About everything. Damn, I spiral fast.

I lean into him, place my head on his chest and close my eyes drinking him in. His smell of lavender and mint soothes my frayed nerves. He rubs my back in soothing circles. God, why can't everything be this simple?

'You worried about going home to see your parents tomorrow?'

I nod, still not moving from his cosy chest.

'Don't worry. I'll be with you.'

Just knowing he still plans on coming with me has me feeling more relaxed.

'If your parents are dicks, I'll just punch them in the face and get us out of there.'

I can't help but laugh. 'You promise?'

'Yep. I'll even get us a Maccy D's on the way home.'

Sunday 11th November

Tom

Man, I felt better after hugging Alice yesterday. It guts me to think of her upset, especially if it's over me. I know the guys told me to stay away from her, but how can I? We live together for God's sakes. That and I can't seem to stay away from her. There's just something about her I can't leave alone.

To say I'm intrigued to meet her parents is an understatement. She's so bloody nervous about today and I have no idea why. I mean, me and my old man are hardly best mates, but I don't carry that sort of anxiety around with me. How bad can they really be?

She's still willing to see them on her mum's birthday, so they can't have done anything awful like beat her. I guess I'll just have to see. I am actually feeling edgy, which Alice keeps teasing me about. I enjoy her teasing me.

I've shaved, showered, and ironed a shirt especially for the occasion. They might be dicks, but I still want to make a good first impression.

'You ready?' Alice asks with a weak smile. She's dressed in a mustard coloured top with a peter pan collar, a maroon cardigan, and a matching tartan full skirt. I still don't get how someone can dress like a grandma and still turn me on so much.

'Babe, you know we don't even have to go, right?'

She smiles adorably. 'What? After you got all dressed up.'

See what I mean about the teasing? She wants in my pants and she doesn't even know it yet.

We drive the forty minutes to their house. Alice finally pulls up outside a large Victorian double fronted property. Wowzas. She didn't mention that her parents are rich.

'This is it,' Alice says as she parks up. She looks up at it in horror.

'So, you're like, rich?' I can't help but ask.

She rolls her eyes. 'Not exactly. My parents come from money. It doesn't mean I have any.'

'But still, you were brought up in this house? In this frigging castle?' I can't keep the shock out of my voice. Rockabilly Alice does not seem like the posh girl I imagined would grow up in a house like this.

She sighs. 'Yeah. I lived here.'

I turn to face her properly. 'Alice, you're worrying me. What did your parents do to you? Am I going to find a cellar with chains or something?'

She frowns before bursting out laughing. 'You've totally got the wrong end of the stick here. My parents aren't monsters or anything like that. They're just... different to me. You'll see.'

She opens the car door and gets out. God, she drives me mad sometimes. I begrudgingly follow her to the large oak door. She squares her shoulders and knocks on the door.

A tall, blonde woman answers the door. She has her hair up in a bun showing off what must be a freshly botoxed face. She's wearing a tweed dress with flat shoes. Who is this bird?

'Alice,' she nods with a tight smile.

She must be a maid or something to greet her so icily.

'Mother,' Alice says with an equally tight smile.

No fucking way! This is her mum? That's how they greet each other? Weird.

'This is my friend Tom I told you about.'

The woman turns as if noticing me for the first time. She looks me up and down shamelessly. I squirm under her scrutiny.

'I don't remember you telling me you were bringing anyone for dinner?' she says while still looking at me inquisitively.

Alice rolls her eyes. 'Yes, I did tell you.'

'Well, we'll see if we can get another place setting laid out.' She turns and walks down the black and white tiled hallway.

Okay... so I'm starting to see why Alice was dreading this.

Alice turns to flash me a grimace before following her mum down the hallway. I plod along after her, already dreading my decision to come here.

I follow them into an old-fashioned living room. It's like a room out of *Antiques Roadshow*. All mahogany furniture and red-striped wallpaper. I can't believe someone as trendy and current as Alice comes from such an old-fashioned house. Growing up here must have killed her.

'We have an extra visitor,' her mum says to her dad, who appears from behind a mahogany bar in the corner holding two sherries. He also scans me over from head-to-toe, but then smiles, appearing friendly.

'Nice to meet you, old chap,' he says, giving a glass to her mum and then using his free hand to slap me on the back. 'Are you and Alice knocking boots?'

'Dad!' Alice shrieks from behind me.

Her dad doesn't look embarrassed at all. 'No shame in it, Alice. We'd just be glad to have you finally off our hands.' He throws his head back on a chuckle as if he's hilarious.

'I'm already off your hands,' she says through gritted teeth. 'I stand on my own two feet.'

'That you do,' her mum says with a snarl. 'At your insistence.'

What's up with that?

I have to change the subject. You can cut the atmosphere with a knife.

'So... something smells nice,' I say rocking awkwardly on my heels. 'What time's dinner?'

Her mum's eyes narrow. 'I'll go ask Marie.'

I look at Alice with raised eyebrows. So, she does have a maid.

'The cook,' she says with an eye roll.

'Bloody hell, your majesty,' I whisper in her ear. 'I didn't realise I was living with royalty.'

She crosses her arms and starts absentmindedly scratching at her forearm. I take her hand to stop her. She looks down at it but not back up at me.

'Dinner's ready,' Alice's mum says poking her head through the door.

Chapter 20

Alice

I woke up feeling more positive about everything. Tom being so sweet to me yesterday had released tons of pent up tension I didn't even realise I was carrying over it. But I had to ruin it by going to my parents' house. I don't even know why I feel I owe these people anything, but if I don't go, I'll just get a load of guilt texts from Mum. It's easier to just go.

But I didn't bank on Tom following through on his promise and coming with me. Now that he's here I can't help but feel awful for putting him through this. The poor guy isn't even sleeping with me.

We make our way into the dining room and take our seats.

'Your brother will be down in a minute,' Mum says, her eyes shining whenever she talks about him. I don't know why. He dropped out of uni and lives through the bank of mum and dad. Just because he occasionally goes to charity balls with them and joins in talking shit with all of those pompous arseholes, they seem to think he's the bee's knees. I'm just some outcast.

I've always felt overshadowed by him, even though I'm

the oldest. I was always the meek, agreeable daughter that kept her head down and went along with everything. Only after breaking up with my first boyfriend, I decided I was sick to death of being treated like a doormat.

Mum's face when I dyed my hair and changed my clothes was a picture. She actually asked me if I was having some sort of nervous breakdown. Called Doctor Reynolds and asked him to assess me. When I got my first tattoo she threatened to have me committed. That's when I knew I could never move back home after uni.

Marie brings in the roast dinner. I take some of the dishes off her and place them down. She's always sweating from the unbearable pressure my parents put on her. Mum's not even flinching, just drinking her sherry and pouring a glass of red wine out for herself.

'So how old's your brother?' Tom asks with a forced smile. He's drinking the red wine Mum's poured for him even though I know he'd prefer a beer.

'Twenty-one, but with a mental age of twelve.'

'Someone talking about me?' We all turn to see Gerald at the door grinning like the Cheshire cat. He's always been a smug little bastard. Mum and Dad have been far too soft on him.

He swaggers into the room and sits down across from me. 'Hey, Ali.'

Ugh, I hate when he calls me Ali.

'Hi,' I say curtly.

He grabs the plate of mashed potato and starts chucking some onto his even though no-one had started. We're all too polite, unlike him, the idiot.

'You're wearing a lot of clothes today, Ali.'

I frown, looking down at my outfit. I'm wearing no more clothes than I normally would. What the hell is he talking about?

I stare back at him. He's grinning at me, his eyes daring me to ask him. Wait... does he know about the pictures? About my nude fucking pictures? Bile starts rising up my throat at the idea of my own brother not just knowing about it, but potentially seeing it.

'What are you on about, Gerald?' Mum snaps. 'She's dressed quite appropriately. Well,' she sighs, 'if it wasn't for all of those tattoos marring her body.' She looks at me pointedly. 'You look like a bloody sailor.'

Dad nods. 'My offer to pay for laser removal still stands.'

'I actually like her tattoos,' Tom says, taking a sip of wine.

Everyone stops to stare at him, as if horrified he not only dare speak, but also dares to disagree with them.

'Sorry, but who are you?' Gerald asks rudely. God, I wish it was still appropriate for me to push him down the stairs.

Tom meets his judging stare with an icy glare of his own. 'I'm Tom.'

'I wasn't asking your name,' Gerald sneers. 'I was asking who you are to Alice?'

Well that's a question and a half.

'I'm her friend and roommate. Oh, and her doggy daddy.'

I burst out laughing, red wine spraying onto the tablecloth.

'For goodness' sake, Alice!' Mum snaps, calling Marie into the room to clean it up.

'What Tom means is that we adopted a dog,' I quickly explain.

Mum's lip curls up in disgust. 'A dog, darling? In that tiny flat of yours? Are you insane?'

Jesus, why is it always my mother's first reaction to

want me locked up in a loony asylum? She's the reason I have anxiety.

'Our dog fits in our life fine, thank you very much.'

'How did you meet?' Gerald asks, leaning back in his chair cockily. 'No, wait. Let me guess. You saw her picture online and answered the ad.'

Oh my god, the bastard is toying with me. Dangling the information in front of Mum and Dad, knowing it will make me squirm.

Tom frowns in confusion, obviously thinking Gerald's a random dickhead. 'No actually. We met on holiday a while back. Our friends are together.'

'Ah, how sweet,' Dad says on a hiccup. 'Young love.' He turns to Mum. 'Do you remember when we were like that, darling? So bright-eyed and bushy-tailed.'

'Yes, yes,' Mum says with a dismissive wave. 'It was wonderful.'

Tom turns to stare at me, his face full of unanswered questions.

'Excuse us for a moment,' Tom says calmly, standing up and taking my hand. Shit, he's going to interrogate me.

He drags me through to the kitchen where Marie is washing some pots. She quickly goes back to what she's doing as if she hasn't seen us.

'Alice, what the hell is your brother going on about?' he demands; his eyes looking over my face, as if already expecting me to talk myself out of it.

'Hmm?' I look around the room, as if it's no big deal.

'Don't fuck around, Alice.' He takes my upper arms and shakes me slightly until I'm looking up at him. 'You know exactly what's going on. Tell me.'

Oh God. I really didn't want him to know this about me.

'Just... my brother's found out something about me and

he's using it to piss me off. Threatening to let my parents know.'

'Okay, I can see that for myself. But what is it? What's so bad you're letting him talk to you like that? What has your face paler than normal?'

Shit, I thought I was getting away with it.

I take a deep breath. 'Okay, but if I tell you, I want you to promise three things.'

He rolls his eyes and crosses his arms over his chest. 'Okay, what are these promises?'

'One, you have to promise not to tell anyone.' He nods. 'Two, you have to promise not to look at me differently.' He frowns, mulls it over and then nods. 'And third you have to not overreact and go mental.'

'Jesus, Alice, just spit it out. Have you killed someone or something?'

I look over at Marie who's definitely listening. I take his arm and drag him out to the garden. I push him against some vines growing up the wall.

'Okay.' One more deep breath. It won't be that bad. Just rip the Band-Aid off and tell him. 'My ex-boyfriend posted naked pictures of me for revenge.'

He remains completely still, not an inch of a muscle moving for exactly four seconds. Then his eyes fall closed. When they open, they're ablaze with rage.

'Your ex posted private pictures of you?' he asks, his chest heaving heavily. I nod. 'Why the hell haven't you called the police?'

'I have, but it's hard for them to trace it back to him, and to be honest with you, I think they have more important things to deal with rather than some silly slut who made a ginormous mistake.'

'What mistake?' he snorts. 'To trust your boyfriend?'

Wow, I can't believe he's taking this so well. To not

completely judge me and tell me it's my fault for being stupid enough to trust someone.

'I want to know where he lives,' he demands.

'No.' I shake my head. 'I'm not having you getting into trouble over me. It's not worth it.'

'That's where you're wrong, Alice.' He takes my face in his hands. 'You are worth it.'

I pause at his words, looking up into his emerald green eyes. Does he really mean that? Does he really value me as more than a piece of arse?

'Well, well, well,' Gerald says, appearing from nowhere. 'Would you look at the sexual tension between you and dog boy.'

'Watch it, dickhead,' Tom warns, his hands clenching into fists.

'Or what?' Gerald asks, clearly having no idea what Tom can do.

In one swift moment Tom has him pinned against the wall. 'You think this is funny?' he snarls into Gerald's face. 'You should be acting like a protective brother and offering to go around this twat's house and sort him out. Not trying to embarrass your sister over it. What kind of man are you?'

Gerald rolls his eyes.

'What on earth is going on here?' We all turn to see Dad and Mum looking on at us in horror. 'Unhand my son!'

Gerald flashes us both a snide smile before turning back to them. 'Dad, this absolute brute was threatening me in my own home. Told me to give him my wallet.'

Tom's nostrils flare in rage.

'No, he fucking didn't!' I scream, completely outraged on his behalf. For him to come out with such a blatant lie; it makes me want to murder him.

'Alice!' Mum berates. 'No swearing in this house.'

'God, that rule is ridiculous, Mother. We're not teenagers anymore. Maybe if you stopped treating Gerald like one he'd get off his arse and get a fucking job!'

'That is enough from you, young lady. We've had enough of your alternative lifestyle.'

'Excuse me?' I ask with a sarcastic laugh. Alternative lifestyle? Anyone would think I'm in a cult.

'Your tattoos, your hair, these insane outfits, your refusal to eat meat. And now this horrid man. Bringing him into our home when you know he's really trying to steal the silver.'

'Mum... you...' I stop myself mid-sentence knowing that no matter what I say I'm not going to change them. They'll never see me for me, just the tattooed disappointment they always have. 'You know what, Mum? I love you, but you're toxic for me. I'm out of here.'

I turn and bolt towards the door.

'You can't just run out of here on my birthday!' Mum shouts behind me.

'Of course she can,' Tom says, quickly running into step with me. 'And your son's a dick.'

Gerald runs up to him. 'At least I'm not a whore who got my tits out for porn!'

Mum shrieks as if someone's been shot. I turn away from them, headed for the door. All I can think about right now is getting out of here. Getting into the car and driving home to my safe place. Only then I hear a smack. I turn to see that Tom has smashed Gerald in the face and he's lying stunned on the floor.

'Get out of my house!' Dad yells.

'Gladly,' Tom retorts taking my hand and pulling me out of the door.

My hero.

Alice

As soon as I'm in the car, I burst into tears. I automatically got into the passenger seat, hoping Tom would drive. He starts the engine and tears out of the drive and down the road.

'Tell me where he lives,' he demands, his eyes still on the road. The veins in his arms raised from what I'm guessing is agitation.

'Huh?'

'Your bastard ex who posted the pictures,' he snaps, not pausing to look at me. 'Where the fuck does he live?'

God, this is typical Tom all over. Just when I need comforting, he's only interested in smashing someone's skull in.

'I'm not telling you,' I cry. 'Just take me home.'

'I'll find out, Alice,' he warns, turning to look at me, his eyes ablaze with rage. 'It'll be a hell of a lot easier if you just tell me.'

'For who?' I scoff. 'For you? Well, sorry if I don't want you to end up in prison.'

He growls, running his hand through his hair. 'God, Alice, you're frustrating as fuck.'

'I doubt you'd let me report your boss for her sexual harassment, so why should you be allowed to butt into my life?'

I've got him there. He frowns but doesn't reply.

I turn my body away from him and look out of the window.

Forty minutes later we pull into our road. I barely wait for the car to stop before I'm unclicking my seat belt and jumping out of the car. I let myself into the flat and attempt to slam the door behind me, but it's caught by Tom.

'Alice,' he snaps from behind me.

I turn to him on a sigh. 'What?'

I've barely got the word out before he's grabbing me, pulling me into his chest and crushing his lips against mine. What the hell? My body goes numb in complete and utter shock. If I ever thought Tom would kiss me, I would have bet a thousand pounds it wouldn't have been in this moment.

I allow myself a moment to savour it before my hands find his hair and fist a clump of it between my fingers. He growls into my mouth. I gasp, allowing his tongue to sneak in.

He pushes me up against the wall, his hands roaming from my waist, down to my arse, then up again until they're palming my breasts through my top. I moan into his mouth. Jesus, since when have I moaned at a bit of petting?

I claw at his shirt, needing his hot skin against me. He helps me unbutton it rashly. In the hurry he loses a button. I couldn't give a fuck right now. I need him naked, like yesterday. He's finally released from it, allowing me to run my palms down along his muscles.

Tom kisses me, then bites down on my bottom lip pulling it out so far, I end up going with it.

He chuckles. 'Your turn.' He takes the edge of my top and whips it off over my head so quickly I feel my hair go static. He's unclipped my bra in record time and has one of my petite boobs in his mouth. I don't even have time to feel self-conscious about their size. Never has a man made me feel so wanted. I suppose he is a professional.

He unzips my skirt. I push him away and attack his jeans. I fumble with the zipper, my shaking hands unable to perform a basic function. I don't know why I'm going so fast. Wait, yes, I do. It's because if we both stop to think this through for more than two seconds we'll realise it's a bad idea.

No time for thinking.

I finally tug them down just as he pushes my skirt to the ground. He walks me backwards into his bedroom, so quickly that he actually trips over his jeans that are still around his ankles. He crushes me to the floor making us both explode in laughter.

Picking me up, he throws me onto the bed. He pauses for a second to look over my body in just my French lacy knickers, the most devilish glint in his eyes. The promise of what's to come. It's the sexiest sight I've ever seen.

If the size of his penis is anything to go by, this is gonna be fucking amazing. He lays back over me, his fingers stroking me lightly. I'm embarrassed by how utterly soaked for him I am.

Without any more preamble, he wiggles out of his boxer shorts, positions himself and thrusts into me. I scream out from being filled to the brim. Fuck me, it feels amazing. All our pent-up energy is finally getting released in the most wonderful way I can think of.

We find an easy rhythm. Each thrust only makes me want more of him. It's wild, and it's frantic, but he still manages to kiss me on my neck, my earlobe, and stroke my hair.

His movements turn frenzied, thrusting inside me relentlessly, grabbing my thigh and yanking it to the side and above so he's even deeper. So deep I cry out, as if in pain, but my god is it the most beautiful kind of pain.

A delicious throb takes hold of me deep down low, vibrating to the pit of my stomach. With each thrust the sensation gets stronger until my whole body is buzzing just for him, needy and begging him to give me the release I need.

I grab onto his arse cheeks, desperate to make it somehow even deeper. His movements become rigid until finally I explode all around him, my body no longer able to hold it in. I mumble something incoherently as my mind hums with warm pleasure. He releases into me shortly after. I barely notice. I'm too busy being sated as fuck.

He lies next to me, both of us panting.

'So...' I begin, out of breath, 'that happened.'

He grins deliciously, his eyes alight with something I haven't seen in them before. Maybe it's lust.

'Yep. And I fucking well enjoyed it.'

I burst out laughing. 'Yeah, I don't know if you noticed, but I did too.' God, I can't believe I came so hard.

He chuckles. 'I think the whole building noticed, to be fair.'

I grimace, covering my face with my hands in an attempt to hide. 'Was I loud?'

'Err... is the Pope Catholic? Of course you were loud. You were being fucked by Tom Maddens. It was never going to be a quiet affair.'

Oh God. I've slept with a man whore. And without a condom. I've got the implant, so I'm not worried about an unplanned pregnancy, but this guy has slept with half of the population. How am I to know he doesn't have something?

'You're clean right?' I can't help but ask.

He scoffs. 'Of course I'm clean.'

'But, like... you've been tested recently?' I clarify. Just in case he's thinking I'm asking if he showered this morning.

'Yeah,' he nods with a squint, like I'm mad for even bringing it up.

'How long ago?'

'Jesus, Alice.' He sighs. 'Only last month. Talk about a way to kill the vibe.'

Oh shit, now I feel bad.

'Sorry, I just had to ask.' I smile up at him.

'No, it's cool. Sorry, I snapped.' He pulls me into his arms for a hug. It's such a simple gesture, but it warms my heart.

'It's fine. We're fine,' I say shyly.

He tucks me under his chin. 'We are.'

Now we just have to figure out where we go from here.

Chapter 21

Tuesday 13th November

Tom

I'm ready to find and kill that cunt that shared those naked pictures of Alice. Now that I've seen her naked myself, I don't want anyone else to see what's mine. Those pictures were private, and this dickwad thinks he can share it with the world? Well, he's got another think coming.

Her idiot of a brother should have been tracking him down too rather than just trying to belittle her. If I ever meet that tool again he'll definitely get a smack on his jaw.

I knew as soon as it happened that I'd get no information from Alice. And we've been kind of busy anyway. That woman is insatiable. So, I've decided I'm getting the info from Jack.

As soon as he enters the gym I sprint on over to him.

'Jack, I need to know which fucker shared those photos.'

Jack's eyes widen, and he scratches his head. 'And hello to you too.'

Now that I look closer I see he still has sleep in his eyes. I suppose it is six am.

'Look, I know you're tired, but wake up, man. I need the name and address of Alice's ex and I need it now.'

He yawns, completely unimpressed by my urgency. 'Speak to Nic. He says he couldn't work it out. Nothing to do with me. I'm just here to work out.'

'Ugh, I'm too stressed for the gym. I'm going to call Nicholas.'

I'm already dialling his number. I don't care if its six am. I've waited long enough. I need to find out what's going on.

'Hello?' he croaks after letting it ring eight times. The lazy bastard.

'Hey, Nic, wake up,' I say loudly. 'I need to know where Alice's fucker ex lives so I can beat the shit out of him.'

He snorts. 'Very mature, Tom. All that will do is get you arrested.'

'I don't give a fuck right now. I need to find him and if you don't help me someone else will.'

He sighs. 'Fine, but I'm coming with you. I'll drive down today, and we can go around there tonight.'

'Fine,' I relent begrudgingly. 'But drive fast.'

Eight torturous hours later we're driving to the address Nicholas gave me.

'Why haven't you and Jack been round here already? Don't you care about Alice?' I still can't believe they both knew and didn't tell me. I get that Alice was embarrassed, but I wouldn't have ribbed her over something as serious as this.

'Of course I do!' he says, as if hurt by the accusation. 'I told Jack and the girls I couldn't trace the IP address, so they'd drop it. I just knew it would cause more trouble.'

'Are you fucking kidding me?' I screech, pulling into a parking space by the block of flats he apparently lives in.

'I crashed the site instead. I checked today, and it's not up anymore.'

'Ugh, how many times have you seen Alice's tits?'

He bursts out laughing. 'Dude, is that the only thing you're concerned about right now?'

'No,' I grunt. Even to my own ears I sound like a brat. 'But I don't like you looking at my bird's tits.'

'Sorry?' he smiles, his eyebrows bunching together 'but did you just say your bird?'

Oh shit. We haven't discussed whether we'll tell the others yet.

'Well... look, let's just get this out of the way, shall we?' I'm getting out of the car before he has a chance to reply.

Someone's leaving the block, so I do a weird kind of run/skip thing and thank the woman. She gives me a flirtatious smile. Of course she does, they all want this.

We take the stairs up to number twelve in silence.

'Are you sure you want to do this?' Nic asks me, chewing on his lip.

I snort and knock at the door, unsure what I'm even going to say. Just that I'm furious. This guy had Alice, and he chose to piss all over that and humiliate her all over the internet.

The door opens and there stands a tall slim guy with a tattoo on his neck, those weird hole things in his ears, and a big quiff. He looks like a fucked-up version of Danny Zuko from Grease. Alice's taste is horrendous. Thank God she finally saw sense when she found me.

'Hi?' he says, looking between us.

'Hi,' I smile, pushing past him and into the flat. The whole place is grotty at best. It makes me appreciate how nice and clean Alice keeps ours. I should thank her for that really.

'Sorry, do I know you?' he asks, eyeing me up and down. He gulps, clearly taking in my size.

My shoulders square. 'No, you know my friend Alice.'

His face falls, and he suddenly doesn't look so confident. He folds his arms across his chest.

'So, what is it you want from me?'

'What I want is a fucking explanation as to how you think that kind of shit is okay?' I bark out, my nostrils flaring.

He sighs, rubbing the back of his neck. 'Look, man, you don't know. The girl threw up on my junk and then dumped me.'

She threw up on him? Good girl. At least she got that in the last time she saw him.

'Look, I don't care how disgusting your dick is, mate. What you did was fucking vile and you need to apologise to her.'

He rolls his eyes. 'Yeah, that's not gonna happen.'

I look to Nicholas and give him the nod. Nic looks back blinking rapidly.

'I was hoping you were going to be more reasonable, but you've left us no choice.'

I punch him in the face, knocking him off his feet and onto his back. Nicholas springs into action and holds him down.

'Nic, pull his jogging bottoms down!' I yell while he struggles to escape.

'What?' he shrieks. 'Why the fuck do you want me to do that?'

'Just do it, Nic!' I shout, getting my phone out.

'I can't!' he shouts back. 'He's wiggling too much.'

Oh, for fuck's sake. I grab his jogging bottoms and pull

them down, along with his boxer shorts, exposing his small limp dick.

'Oh my god, Tom,' Nicholas says, looking away. 'What the fuck are you going to do to him?'

'Don't rape me!' the dickhead ex screams. 'I'll do anything.'

'I'm not going to rape you, you twat.'

I put my phone to camera and snap a picture of his pathetic penis.

'What the hell are you doing?' he shouts, bucking Nicholas off and going to grab the phone.

'Uh, uh, uh,' I pout unable to hide my grin. 'It's only fair that everyone gets to see your dick too.'

'Come on, bro,' he tries to reason with me, his eyes desperate. 'You know what chicks are like. She fucked me over.'

I grit my teeth. 'I don't care if she fucked your father, you don't do this to a girl. And as for emailing it round to all of her clients, well that's even more fucked up.'

He wrinkles his forehead. 'What are you talking about? I never sent any emails.'

I snort a laugh. 'Quit the bullshit. We know exactly what you've done.'

'Listen, I never sent any emails, I swear! I just uploaded it to that site when I was pissed off.'

I look at his features, trying to work out if he's lying, which he'd be a dick to do at this point. Could he really be telling the truth? I glance to Nicholas. He nods, as if to confirm that he believes him.

'Okay, so if it wasn't you, who did it?'

'I've no idea.' He puts his palms up in surrender. 'I swear to God.'

Dammit. Then who the fuck sent it around?

'Okay, fine. I believe you.' I nod to Nicholas and we turn to leave.

'Wait! Are you still going to post the photo?' he asks, his arms wrapped around himself.

I smile smugly. 'You didn't think you were gonna get away with it that easily, did you?'

Wednesday 14th November

Alice

We've spent the last couple of days having sex around the flat. Poor Pickles keeps looking at us with her head turned to the side. My God, the sex is hot, just as Brooke promised. But one glaringly obvious thing hanging over us is that we've not discussed if this is a proper relationship or just a friends-with-benefits situation.

It's Nicholas' thirtieth birthday tonight so we're all going out for dinner. He insisted he didn't want a party. A mid-week meal was the craziest he'd allow Brooke to organise. She's booked us into a Chinese restaurant that has a private back room you can hire. I'm sure he'll still groan over that.

It's the first time I'm seeing Molly since I lost it and told her I knew she was into Charlie. I haven't spoken to her since. She hasn't even sent me her occasional happy quotes to make me smile. She must be really upset.

Tom and I are nearly at the restaurant and still neither of us have brought up how we're going to act in front of everyone. I'm sweating at the thought of it. I know they're going to grill me about it.

Another thing I can't stop worrying about is if Tom

was telling the truth about being clean. I mean, he'd have no reason to lie, right?

We're the first at the table. I sigh a massive sigh of relief. If we'd have walked in hand in hand, they would have pounced on us.

Brooke has decorated the wood panelled room with a huge thirty balloon, streamers, and I don't doubt she has a personalised cake out back for him.

I order a large wine and fiddle with the rings on my fingers.

'Why do you look so nervous?' Tom asks with a bemused look on his face.

'No reason!' I shrill loudly. Way to play it cool Alice.

He opens his mouth to say something when Molly comes rushing in looking flustered.

'Sorry! Sorry I'm late,' she says, taking her coat off to sit down. 'I am just absolutely manic organising this charity night at the zoo. You'd be surprised how much work it is. You're still coming, right?'

'Of course,' I smile. I've taken the animal pictures for their website thanks to Molly, so I like to keep my foot in the door. 'I can even take a few shots if you like?' I offer, as way of an apology for being a bitch the last time she saw me.

'Really?' she asks, eyes wide with excitement. 'That would be amazing!'

No, Molly is amazing. She never holds a grudge after an argument. The girl is pure sunshine.

'Of course.'

Evelyn, Erica, and Jack are the next ones in. Brooke's always late. We exchange kisses and talk about what we plan to wear to Molly's charity do at the zoo. Charlie comes in still wearing his suit from work. He's got the next two days off, so he can relax tonight without worrying about driving back to Peterborough.

Brooke and Nicholas are next in. He's wearing a giant lit up badge saying, 'Hug me, I'm thirty.' The poor guy.

'Sorry, bitches, but my hair just wouldn't co-operate,' she says as she breezes in. 'But I finally have the birthday boy.' The minute she spots me she freezes. 'Oh my god, you had sex,' she blurts out.

I spit out some of my wine.

'What?' I shriek, feeling my cheeks heating up. Do not go red. Do not go red.

'You totally have!' she insists, taking off her red trench coat.

Do not look at Tom. Whatever the hell you do, do not look at him.

'How on earth can you tell that?' Erica asks, looking between us.

'It's obvious,' she chuckles. 'She might as well have it tattooed on her forehead.' She pulls out the chair. 'Now come on, I want deets!'

'No way!' Molly says clapping excitedly. She turns to Tom. 'Were you the lucky man?'

Evelyn rolls her eyes. 'Please tell me you bunked up with a total stranger and didn't shag that manwhore?'

Tom glares back at Evelyn but doesn't say anything.

'What, you'd rather I sleep with a stranger than Tom?' I look to Tom and give him a shy but encouraging smile.

'Yeah, that's crazy logic,' Erica laughs, 'even for you.'

'Whatever,' she snorts. 'Just don't come crying to me when it all goes tits up.'

'Evelyn!' Brooke snaps. 'Stop being such a Debbie Downer and just listen, will you?'

'Yeah, tell us everything,' Molly coos, leaning in.

'There is nothing to tell!' I insist feeling my cheeks heat. 'Now, can we please go back to enjoying Nic's birthday?'

'Yeah,' Nicholas says. 'I'm feeling very birthday diva right now,' he says sarcastically. I smile back at him, grateful for the help.

I look back at four intrigued faces, eagerly waiting for me to spill. The moment the guys are out of earshot, they're going to be grilling me.

We go about ordering our food and chatting random shit. I excuse myself to go to the toilet. As soon as I'm walking, I hear the girls make the same excuse. Damn it, they're after me.

I walk into the toilets and lean against the sink, ready for the onslaught. A poster for a vintage fair catches my eye. Sometimes I wish I had friends that were into the same things, but I've dragged these girls to one too many vintage fairs over the years.

The door bangs closed behind me and all of them stare expectantly, their eyes wide in excitement. Well, Evelyn's is in disgust.

'Guys, it's private.'

I'm not like Brooke. I don't openly discuss my sex life. Another reason why I was so mortified when those pictures came out.

'No fun!' Brooke protests.

'Well, at least tell us how it happened?' Erica pleads, her eyes wide and desperate.

I feel my cheeks flush.

'Oh my god,' Molly coos, 'you are *so* in love.'

I push her on the shoulder. 'Shut up. I'm not in love with Tom 'Manwhore' Maddens.'

Evelyn snorts. 'Well, at least you still have *some* of your brain still intact.'

'Purlease,' Brooke laughs, 'I'm sure he fucked all the sense out of you!'

I cringe. 'Brooke!' we all shriek, before collapsing into hysterical laughter.

They all keep looking at me expectantly.

'Ugh, okay, fine. So, I took him to my parents for dinner.'

'Whoa!' Erica stops me. 'He's already met the parents? Is this serious?'

I shake my head. 'It wasn't like that. Anyway, it's a long story, but we left my parents after they were arseholes and Tom found out about the photos. He was demanding to know his address and then it just kind of... happened.'

'Oh em gee!' Molly shrieks. 'He went all burly caveman on you. That is SO sweet!'

I roll my eyes but can't stop from laughing.

'You didn't tell him, did you?' Erica asks with concern.

'Of course not.'

'Good,' Evelyn nods. 'God knows he'd only go and get himself arrested. Not that I can blame him for wanting to carve his dick off. I've had similar thoughts myself.'

We all crack up laughing.

'I take it I can count on you both for Friday's zoo charity event then?' Molly asks, shifting nervously from foot to foot.

'Babe, stop worrying. I keep telling you we're coming.'

'Sorry.' She chews on her lip. 'I'm just bricking it. Worried something is going to go wrong.'

I'm pleased at the change of subject.

'You'll be fine, Molls,' Erica says with a supportive hand on her shoulder.

'So, have you had the awkward chat yet?' Erica asks, squirming at the thought.

'Awkward chat?' I repeat, confused. Ugh, she's talking about me and Tom again.

'Yeah,' she nods, 'about whether you're exclusive. Whether you're boyfriend and girlfriend.'

I cringe. 'God, the whole thing is just so mortifying. I'm not having any such stupid chat with Tom. I'm just taking it day by day.'

'Okay,' Brooke nods, 'but this is Tom we're talking about. Maybe specify the only having sex with you part.'

I know she's right, but it doesn't stop me being a wimp. The others go for a wee, but Molly applies some lip gloss in the mirror.

'Molly, I'm so sorry about what I said at the school fair,' I whisper so the others can't hear.

She shrugs. 'It's fine. If I'm honest, you might be right. I just… I've got a lot on at the moment. I don't have time to be having a sexual identity crisis like this at the minute.'

'Okay, well, what I meant to say is that I'm here for you, whenever you want to talk about it.'

She smiles. 'Thanks, Alice.'

I go to have a wee myself. I wait until I can only hear Brooke's heels by the sink before escaping the cubicle.

'So, go on,' she leans in. 'What's up?'

She knew I wanted to talk to her about something. I swear, sometimes she's telepathic.

'I did a stupid thing,' I admit with a grimace.

She snorts a laugh. 'Well, yeah, you slept with Tom, but don't worry, it happens to the best of us.' She winks.

'No, not just that. The first time we did it… well,' I swallow, 'we kind of got caught up in the moment.'

She raises her eyebrows. 'You mean you didn't use a johnny with Tommy?'

I cover my face with my hands. 'Uh, don't joke about

it. This is serious.' My chest feels so tight whenever I think about it.

'Jesus, what is it with you and Erica? I used to sleep around, but I always made sure I used a condom.'

'Okay, enough of the lecture from queen slag herself.'

'Hey!' she shouts, throwing her paper towel at me. 'I'm reformed!'

I smile. 'Sorry. But, regardless. Look, I've got the implant, but I'm worried Tom wasn't telling me the truth and might have caught something along the line.'

'Well, yeah, he's a manwhore,' she agrees with a nod.

'I know.' I start chewing my nails. 'So, will you... come to the clinic with me?'

'Of course, babe. Have you not been before?' she asks, as if every girl dreams of going there.

'Of course not! I don't make a habit of this.'

She chuckles. 'Okay, chill your boots. We'll go tomorrow. We need to talk business anyway.'

Chapter 22

Thursday 15th November

Alice

I didn't get a chance to chat to Tom last night. Well, more like didn't have the guts. It helped that we were both so knackered we passed out as soon as we got in. Not even sex. Maybe he's already bored with me.

I'm woken by gentle kisses on my shoulder.

'Wake up, sleepyhead.'

I begrudgingly open my eyes to see his clear green eyes looking down at me with something like adoration. He's holding a cup of tea and some toast. Wow, he's a keeper. Who knew I'd ever imagine Tom 'Manwhore' Maddens being a keeper? I suppose stranger things have happened. Like dinosaurs.

I sit up, eager for the tea. 'Wow, thanks. Did you use the vegetarian butter?' I can't help but check.

'Yes,' he smiles with a shake of his head.

'What's this all in aid of?' I can't help but be suspicious that he's already fucked-up.

'Just wanted to treat you.' He smiles, too good-looking to want little old me.

I pretend to sniff the air. 'And the kitchen isn't on fire, right?'

He pretend punches me on the same shoulder he was kissing a minute ago. 'Ha ha.' He sits down next to me folding his legs underneath him. 'Actually, there was something I wanted to tell you.'

Uh-oh. My stomach drops. This is it. When he lets me down. When he shows me he is the manwhore I've always expected him to be. He's cheated on me already, or maybe he just wants to end this. Or make sure I realise it's just sex and nothing else. My heart sinks at the idea.

'Okay,' I say with a forced smile. 'What's up?' Sound breezy Alice. Fucking breezy.

'Well... I kind of went to see your ex-boyfriend a few days ago.'

'You what?' I blurt out, completely muddled. 'You went to see my ex?'

He nods. 'That twat that uploaded your picture. Thought he needed a little talking to.'

'How did you even find him?' Did Erica give him his details? I didn't even think I'd told her where he lived.

'No, it was Nicholas that tracked him down. Anyway, we gave him a telling off.'

Visions of him punching him flash through my mind. 'Tom! Tell me you didn't beat him? The police will be here soon to arrest you, you idiot!'

He laughs. 'Don't be stupid. I barely touched him. But I did manage to take this.' He hands over his phone. I press the unlock button to see him lying down with his dick out.

'Oh my god!' I snort a laugh. 'How the hell did you get this picture?'

'We kind of held him down. Anyway, it's now up on the same revenge porn site and it's been emailed out to his employer.'

My stomach drops. 'Shit, what if they're able to trace it to you?'

He smiles smugly. 'You honestly think Nicholas would let me be that stupid? He uploaded it and encrypted the shit out of it. Or whatever the hell it is he does. There's no way to trace it to us.'

I know I should feel happy about this, but... well, it's just another life ruined.

'Hey! Don't you go feeling sorry for that creep. He did this to you.'

'Yeah, but two wrongs don't make a right.'

'Jesus, Alice. You're too good for this world, do you know that?'

I lean over and kiss him. 'I'm too good for him. I'm just right for you.'

He grins. 'Before we get on with some sexy time, I need to tell you. He's adamant that he didn't email out the link to people. Is there anyone else you can think of that would do it? Any other exes you threw up on?'

I burst out laughing. 'No, I can't say there is. He's probably lying anyway. But... will you guys take it down?'

'You're joking, right?'

I shake my head. 'I don't feel good about it. Please, Tom.'

He rolls his eyes and sighs. 'Fine.'

'Also, I want to know if your boss is still making inappropriate passes at you?'

He rolls his eyes. 'Chill, babe. I told her where to go and she's left me alone since. I just needed to stand up to her.'

'Really?'

'Really,' he nods.

He leans me back and starts kissing me passionately. But I can't help but wonder, what if he was telling the truth about someone else sending the email? Who else would do that to me?

***

Alice

After our sexy session, I had a quick shower and now I'm on the way to the family planning clinic with Brooke. I can't help but feel like I'm betraying his trust. It worries me that I've slept with a man I don't trust one hundred percent. Last time I did that I ended up with naked photos of myself all over the internet.

She's stood outside puffing on a cigarette, her forehead unusually furrowed. She only smokes when she's stressed.

'Hey, Brooke, what's up?'

She sighs and stubs it out under her foot.

'Nothing,' she shrugs forcing a smile. 'Now let's get you tested for STI's.'

'Shush!' I snap, looking around to see if anyone heard her. 'I don't want the whole world knowing. And don't give me that bullshit. I see you with your stress cigarettes.'

'Ugh, fine! Nicholas is on about me moving to Peterborough again.'

'You're joking?'

She sighs. 'I wish I was. I can't move there. Do you know what happens to people like me that move to shit places like Peterborough?'

I glare at her. She's only been there a few times.

'They give up. Cease to exist. Next thing you know I've got three kids, a bitchy cat, and a baggy vagina.'

I burst out laughing. She doesn't join me. She looks more worried that it's actually going to happen.

'Brooke, you need to talk it through with Nicholas without slagging off his home town.'

She bites her lip. 'I just don't get why he wouldn't want to move here. I mean it's Brighton for God's sake. Plus, on top of that Erica and Jack are talking about getting their own place. They're sick of me walking in on them doing it.'

'Hi, can I help you?' a lady at the reception desk asks.

'Oh,' I almost forgot where we were for a minute. 'Yes, I'm here to see someone please.'

'Down the hall and sit on the chairs. You're number eighty.' She hands over a ticket.

Wow, there must be a lot of sluts about today. Myself included.

'You'll need to complete this.' She hands over a form clipped to a clipboard.

We take a seat. I have a quick scan over the other people waiting, all of us trying to avoid looking each other in the eye. No-one I recognise, thank god.

'So why doesn't he want to move to Brighton? I thought he could work from anywhere?'

She rolls her eyes. 'Ugh, it's his whole leaving his dad thing again. I mean, I get it. He's all alone, but if he'd just see some of the women he's been matched up with online he'd be far less lonely.'

'You can't force someone to do online dating if they don't want to. He's probably still cut up about losing his wife. I don't think you ever get over that kind of thing.'

'Well, if he'd stop being such a stubborn bastard and look at his matches he might just stand a chance.'

I roll my eyes and complete the form ticking the STI check. I wait as the other numbers are called. Brooke tells me that two of Jack's photos have sold for £600 each. That means I've earnt £480 just for two photos. Who knew this would actually work?

My number is finally called.

'Want me to go in there with you?' she asks with raised eyebrows. 'Hold your hand?'

'I'll be fine,' I say rolling my eyes. We both know I'm lying, but I square my shoulders and follow the lady into the room. She takes my form and scans over it.

'Okay, Miss Watts. Do you mind me calling you Alice?'

The woman is about to look at my vagina. I'm pretty sure we can be on first name terms.

'Fine,' I nod.

'Okay, so you're here for an STI check. I just need to run through some routine questions first.'

I nod again, bracing myself.

'So, in your own words why are you here today?' She smiles kindly.

'Err... for an STI check...?'

She nods, the corners of her mouth upturning ever so slightly. She quickly recovers so as to look professional. 'So, you've had unprotected sex recently?'

'Um...' I clear my throat. 'Yes.'

'Okay, and are you aware if this person already has an STI?'

'No. He said he's been tested, but I'm not sure if he's telling the truth.'

God, I feel like a slut saying that. Admitting that I'm sleeping with someone I don't trust one hundred percent.

'How many people have you had sexual contact with in the last six months?'

Jesus, how is this relevant?

'Just the two.' I'm sure she's used to people saying hundreds.

'Can you describe your last sexual experience?'

I nearly choke on my own tongue. 'Excuse me?' This bitch wants gory details? Wants to know what position we used? Is this even relevant?

'The type of sex,' she clarifies, 'whether it was oral, vaginal or anal.'

'Oh, um, vagina-based.' God, I sound like an idiot. 'But I mean, he has gone down on me too.' God, this is mortifying.

'Do you have one or more sexual partners?'

'No! God, one at a time. Jesus.' The back of my neck is starting to sweat now.

'Please remember that these questions aren't used to judge you. We just need to ask them.'

'Okay,' I nod, squirming in my seat.

'Is your partner of the same gender or opposite?'

'It was a man.'

'Has your sexual partner ever paid for sex?'

My eyes widen. She's asking if Tom's ever had sex with a prostitute? 'Oh my god, no! I mean, shit, I hope not.' Way to sound confident about your sexual partner.

'Is your sexual partner bi-sexual? Has he ever had anal sex with a man?'

'No! Jesus.' My cheeks are burning. I want to get out of here. My heart is beating so fast I can hear it. If it carries on like this, I'm going to be headed for a panic attack.

'Has he ever had sex with an animal?'

'Jesus, of course not! What kind of freaks do you think we are?'

It's my tattoos, isn't it? It's caused her to judge me. People are always the same.

'Just standard questions.' She writes something on her notes. 'Right, here it is.' She hands over a container holding what looks like a long cotton bud.

Hang on a minute. Does she expect me to do it myself?

'Oh... do I do it myself then?' I ask, feeling stupid.

'Yes, in the bathroom.' I stare back at her in disbelief. 'You do know where your vagina is, don't you?' she smiles. Oh, she's taking the piss out of me. Nice.

'Okay.'

I go to the bathroom and insert the cotton bud thing. Wiggle it around inside myself and then put it safely back into the container. I go back in and hand it over to the lady.

'Great, thanks. Now I'll just take a blood test to rule out HIV. If everything comes back fine, we'll send you a text message. If there are any issues, we'll give you a call.'

How can she be so bloody calm about it? In a few days I'm going to know if I'm fine or if the man I'm sleeping with is a liar.

Chapter 23

Saturday 17th November

Alice

I look at myself in the mirror, smoothing down my floral Nancy dress in an array of blues, blacks, and greys, on white cotton. Its sweetheart neckline is flattering to my modest chest, but you want to know the best thing about it? There are hidden pockets in the flared swing skirt. I love pockets on dresses! Somewhere to put your hands when you're feeling awkward. Or to store your lipstick.

Tom sidles up behind me, smoothing his hands over the fabric at my waist and moving them down to my bottom which he gives a slight squeeze.

'You look gorgeous.'

I turn to him in his dark navy suit and white shirt. 'You don't look so bad yourself.'

In fact, he looks fucking delicious. He's so muscular you can make out the curves of his biceps in that jacket. And I hit that. *Yeah, I do!*

We get a taxi to the zoo and follow the signs to the fundraiser, all the while avoiding having the awkward conversation I feel is lingering over us. We enter their conference hall to find it decorated with the huge printed out pictures that I took for their website. Wow, they look good in large, if I do say so myself. Molly is so sneaky. She never said she was doing this.

There are green and yellow balloons dotted around the place with a huge sign that says 'Raise Money for our Animals!'

'Hey, guys!' Molly says, bounding over to us in a pink-sequinned dress better suited to Barbie. Only she could pull it off.

'Hey,' we both smile.

'The guys are all over by the bar. I've got to go schmooze.' She totters off in her heels.

Tom laughs. 'Of course they are.'

We walk over to them. 'Well,' Tom says slapping Jack and Nicholas on the back, 'don't we all look dapper in our suits?' He takes two glasses of Prosecco and hands one to me.

'Where's Pickles?' Evelyn asks.

Did she seriously think we'd bring her?

'Our day care lady has her,' I explain with a nod. 'Keeping her overnight.'

'Hey, guys, I have a question,' Brooke says playfully. On closer inspection her hair is messy and her eyes a bit glassy. God, she's drunk. When did she start drinking? Nicholas straightens himself behind her as if ready to reel her in. 'Are you guys officially together now, or what?'

I freeze, my cheeks heating so much I'm scared they'll actually set on fire. Why the hell is she bringing this up? She knows I want to see how it goes.

'Because it is *exhausting* watching you dance around each other,' she continues before throwing her head back on a laugh.

I notice Tom tensing beside me. Why the hell did she decide getting so smashed this early would be a good idea?

'Alright, Brooke,' Nicholas says. 'I told you to slow down tonight, remember?'

'Jeez, what is the big deal?' she snaps, before turning to glare at Jack. Why is she glaring at Jack? What did he do?

'Brooke, can I have a word?' I ask with a polite smile. I take her arm and start dragging her away from everyone. When I'm pleased we're in a quiet enough corner I start my interrogation. 'What's going on? You never normally get this trashed. This can't just be about Nicholas pressurising you to move, can it? And why are you glaring at Jack?'

She scoffs. 'Because everyone thinks he's fucking perfect and I know better.'

I frown. 'Who, Jack? You know better? Why?'

'He's cheating on Erica,' she blurts out with a hiccup.

My mouth drops open.

'He's WHAT?' I shriek, causing half the hall to turn and stare at me. I wait until the chatter goes back to an acceptable level. 'Why the hell do you think that?'

'I've caught him twice whispering on the phone. The minute he sees me he panics and starts rambling some excuse.'

That's really not strong evidence.

'So, what makes you think he's cheating? He could be talking to anyone.'

'Really?' she raises her eyebrows. 'Even you can't be that stupid.'

'Even me?' I snap. 'What the fuck does that mean?' I hate mean drunks. My own mother is one.

'That you're naive when it comes to men.'

She might as well have slapped me. It stings just the

same. Especially with everything up in the air between me and Tom.

'Admit it, Alice. You have bad taste in men. Tom is no better. I mean, do you even know if you're just fucking friends, or whether he even likes you for real?'

Brooke is never this mean. I hate how she's this drunk.

'Fuck you, Brooke. I'll ask him right now if it stops you chatting shit.'

I spin on my heel and go straight for Tom. I pat him on the shoulder. He turns around with a smile.

'I need to talk to you.' I take his hand and lead him out through the patio doors. We walk through an animal enclosure, the lights dimmed. I'm assuming the animals are asleep.

'Listen, Tom. I have to tell you something.'

Here goes. I look into his green eyes lit up by the moonlight, aware I'm potentially about to break my own heart. Hearing he's not interested in me like that is going to hurt.

'I...' I'm interrupted by a loud barking noise. Shit, they have dogs in this zoo?

'What the hell is that?' he asks, standing in front of me to guard me against the barking dogs I've no doubt are about to be released to kill me. That small gesture tells me he truly cares, regardless of what he's about to say.

The barking goes again, this time followed by a loud, deep 'Eugh!'

'I don't think it's a dog,' I say, standing out in front of him and attempting to follow the sound. I walk down around a corner and find two sea lions yapping away.

'Sea lions,' Tom laughs. 'I had no idea they were such noisy fuckers.'

'Yeah, who knew,' I giggle.

'Anyway, what were you trying to say?'

'Oh, I -'

'EUGHHHHHHH!' they shout again.

He smiles, and it's so beautiful I have to remind myself why I'm trying to ruin this. So, what if he doesn't feel the same way about me? The main thing is that right now we're together. In some capacity at least. Right now, I have him and the thought of letting him go has me gasping for breath.

He takes my hand and pulls me further away from them.

'I just wanted to ask...' I swallow, in an attempt to calm myself, 'if this is real?' I look down at the floor. 'You know, if we're sort of... together, or if we're just like... doing this as friends?' God, I sound like an idiot. I hate myself.

He takes me around the waist, sending tingles up and down my spine. I brace myself to be let down gently.

'Alice, I'm in. Full in.'

He what now? Did I hear him right? He's in?

'Really? And you reckon you're able to have a proper relationship with me?' I ask with a nod, unable to believe him.

'When you put it like that....' he grimaces, before bursting out laughing. 'Yes, Alice. For you, it'll be easy.'

He moves his lips to kiss the corner of my mouth before placing them fully on mine as if they've always belonged there. His hand travels up my spine until they're in my hair, sliding out to frame my jaw.

I kiss him back with everything I've got, as if pouring my feelings into him. Telling him how happy I am that he's willing to try. He's made it sound easy, but I know with him it will be anything but. How can one person change their core personality completely overnight? I dismiss the thought as he breaks the kiss.

We walk back into the hall hand-in-hand just as Molly's finishing her speech.

'And now I'll hand you over to my friend Jack Lawson.'

Jack? What the hell is Jack doing up there? I didn't think he was helping with the charity. He walks up and takes the mike. Erica looks just as baffled as us. Why wouldn't he have told her if he was involved?

'What's he doing?' I whisper to Tom.

'Fuck knows,' he whispers back, looking as anxious as me.

'Right. Hi, everybody. My name is Jack Lawson and I hope you don't mind me sabotaging the evening.'

'Boo!' Brooke heckles, laughing at herself. Nicholas frowns next to her.

Erica's looking panicked now. Charlie's chewing his lip. If anyone knows something its him.

Jack clears his throat. 'Did you know that a family of *Meerkats* is often called a mob, gang, or clan? Well, I wanted to wait until we had our gang together again before I said this.' He looks around at us and smiles. Oh my god, wait. Is he... proposing to Erica? No!

He locks eyes with a very jittery Erica.

'*Elephants* never forget, and I'll never forget the moment I first met you at that little caravan park in Burnham-on-Sea.'

Erica's cheeks turn bright red.

'Erica, you might not have been as tall as a *giraffe*, as graceful as a *gazelle*, or as fabulous as a *flamingo*, but you were as cute and furry as a *panda*.'

Panda? Jesus, someone should have helped him with this speech.

Molly starts giggling. I can basically see Erica wondering if that means she's got too much facial hair.

'I love our *sloth* like lazy Sundays where we *pig* out on takeaways and sweets.'

Erica smiles back at him, slowly calming down the more he talks.

'I know that sometimes you can be as fierce as a *tiger* and sometimes a right moody *cow*. A drama *llama* with the snap of a *crocodile* when you have a big *camel* style hump.

'Well, *sea otters* hold hands when they sleep, so they don't drift away from each other at night. I want to hold your hand every night and wake up with you there every morning.'

Oh my god, this is so sweet. I feel myself tearing up. I want this kind of love. Will Tom ever be capable of this?

'I want you to waddle like a *penguin* when we have our first baby. I don't care if you put on so much weight you turn into a *hippopotamus* or if you turn clingy like a *koala*.

'I'll never be a *cheetah* and I'll try my best not to be a *baboon*. I promise to always stay *foxy* and never be a *snake*.

'So, Erica Bennett, will you hold my otter pocket for eternity? Make me the happiest man in the world and marry me?'

Oh my god, I was right. He wants to marry Erica!

Everyone turns to look at Erica. She's smiling, no… *beaming* at Jack. It's obvious what her answer is even before she speaks.

'Of course, I'll marry you!' she squeals.

Chapter 24

Tom

I can't believe Jack and Erica are getting married. It's insane! I mean, I guess I always knew he was in it long term with her, but marriage is a whole other step and one I thought was a few years away. Just the thought of spending my entire life with someone fills me with dread. To think Jack is ready to take that step scares me.

I look at Alice who's busy washing up after breakfast. Shit, does she want all this eventually too? Am I even able to give her this? I've only ever been good at seducing women. Not having to please them long term. Fuck, I need a shot. Not another day of being pressured by this boss of mine. I've decided that today I'm going to tell her once and for all to back off.

The problem is I've been too polite. Too scared of losing my job to tell her to stop. I think once I stand up for myself and let her know I'm having none of it she'll get embarrassed and back off. Well, that's what I'm hoping for. I need to get it sorted now I've lied to Alice and said I've already done it.

I've been at work fifteen minutes when I feel her behind me. It's like every hair on the back of my neck stands up to attention when she's around. Alert and alarmed at her presence.

'Tom, I've just sent you a spreadsheet. Open it up please.'

I cringe inwardly, begrudgingly opening the attachment. She leans over me, one arm on the back of my chair, the other caging me in. Her slutty perfume completely overpowers me. I have to stifle a cough.

'As you can see,' she says pointing at the screen with her long red nails, but at the same time managing to flash her cleavage. I turn and deliberately keep my eyes on the screen.

She starts waffling on, dragging out her explanation so that she can stay close to me.

'Tom.' I snap back to reality to find her staring at me. She licks her lips suggestively. Her lipstick has run into the lines around her lips. 'Can I see you in my office for a moment?'

Oh God. I've used every excuse possible up to now, to avoid going into her office with her alone. But for the life of me I can't think of a single reason why I can't go with her. Maybe I should just accept my fate. Stop running from it. That's what I came in here to do today; confront her.

I nod and numbly follow her into her bland blue office.

'Shut the door behind you,' she orders as she sits down behind her desk.

I begrudgingly shut it. Keep it together, Tom. She can't do anything to you that you don't want to happen.

'So,' she begins chewing suggestively on a pen. 'How do you think you're getting on working here, Tom?'

I put my hands in my pockets to stop them shaking and

rock on my heels. 'Okay, yeah.' I shrug, wanting to appear laid back and in control.

She stands up and walks slowly towards me. Her walk is predatory, her gaze challenging.

'I'd say your performance has been pretty standard. Under normal circumstances I'd be arranging your P45.'

'But...' I ask, knowing she wants me to bite.

She comes so close I can feel her breath on my ear. 'But I'm sure there are ways for you to improve on your performance.' She leans forward and cups my dick.

I inhale sharply. Fuck. I haven't been imagining it. She's a predator. My dick shrivels in her hand.

'I have a girlfriend,' I blurt out, hoping to God it's enough to get her to leave me the fuck alone.

She smiles cruelly. 'She can't know the tricks I do. Trust me, Tom. With age comes experience.'

I close my eyes, trying to block her out. How can she be so sure of herself? I've never been so repulsed in all my life.

'I'm happy with my girlfriend,' I insist, trying to stand firm. I move away from her, so her hand isn't cupping my dick anymore.

'And how will your little girlfriend feel if you get fired and have to move home to Peterborough?'

My shoulders turn rigid. 'I'll just get another job.'

She laughs cruelly. 'Don't think for a second you'll be getting another job down here. I know a lot of people, Tom. A lot of influential people. You won't stand a chance in this town again. So, I really hope your little girlfriend is ready for a long-distance relationship.'

Fuck, how can this be happening?!

'So, what do you suggest I do?' I ask sarcastically, glaring back at her.

'I suggest you do me,' she grins. I grimace. The woman

has no shame. 'You have until Wednesday to think it over. I hope you come to the right decision. That'll be all.'

Tuesday 20th November

Alice

Tom arrived home last night in a weird mood. He was a bit distant, like he had a lot on his mind. I'm worried Jack proposing to Erica has freaked him out and made him realise that what we have is a lot like a committed relationship.

That could be a lot for a manwhore like Tom to take in, so I decided to give him some space and have a relaxing bubble bath. Well... it would have been relaxing if Pickles hadn't have kept throwing herself against the bathroom door trying to get in.

If I'm honest with myself, seeing Erica so happy with her huge rock of a ring has made me feel jealous. It's not that I want to get married right away, but I'd like to think that it's possible for my future.

It might have helped that Jack picked Erica the most fabulous ring I've ever seen. It's a vintage style white-gold ring with diamonds set all along the band and the most exquisite star shaped diamond.

I mean, I know that I'm always banging on about factory mass-produced jewellery, but this doesn't look it. He's also got it engraved with the date they first talked back on that little caravan holiday.

But today things are looking up. I got a call from the zoo to say that I won the charity raffle. Two tickets to Barcelona! Can you believe it? I'm still in shock. I rang

Molly to double check it wasn't a joke. I've decided that I'm going to surprise Tom when he gets in tonight.

This is just what he needs right now; to see that I'm not an old boring wife type. That we have years of fun ahead of us. Of living our lives to the fullest, just together.

As soon as the key's in the lock, Pickles scuttles around the corner to meet him. I quickly pop on a bit of lipstick. God, look at me. I'm like a bloody stereotypical 1950's wife.

'Hey,' he says as soon as he sees me, a tired smile on his face. He still looks gorgeous. Damn, I've got it bad.

'Hey,' I grin. 'Guess what?'

His eyes wander across my face. 'What?'

'I won the raffle at the zoo. We're going to Barcelona!'

His eyes widen, his smile growing. 'Are you serious?'

'Yep!' I grin, throwing myself into his arms. He instinctively picks me up and spins me around. See, things like this; these things show that we're meant to be. Surely? Anyone that can spin me has to be a win, right?

'I can't believe it. When do we go?'

I grimace. 'That's the only thing. It's this weekend, so I was wondering if you could get a half day Friday? We fly at 6pm, but you know, with checking in and everything...'

'Okay,' he nods, again deep in thought. 'I could ask.'

'Great.'

He presses his lips against me in a kiss so desperate, if I didn't know any better I'd think he was saying goodbye.

Chapter 25

Tom

Last night I made love to Alice. For the first time, actually made love. And damn it, I'm pretty sure I am in fucking love with her. Not that it can continue. After yesterday it's ruined either way.

Either I choose to give in and sleep with my boss, meaning I've cheated and would have to confess. Or I refuse and lose my job and any hope of working in Brighton. I'll have to move back to Peterborough. Sure, we might fool ourselves for a few weeks, but we all know long-distance relationships don't work.

So last night I held her extra tight, marvelled in how soft her skin was, how sweet and innocent she looks when she smiles up at me naked. At how her cheeks flush when she orgasms. God, just thinking about losing her has me clutching my chest, as if I'm having a heart attack. Can you get heartburn from heartbreak? Or is this just what it feels like to lose someone?

I considered telling her how much I've fallen head over heels in love with her last night, but what's the point? It'll only hurt her more when we don't work. Best to just cut my losses, nip it in the bud before it hurts too bad. Who am I kidding? I haven't even done it yet and already I feel sick to the stomach.

I walk as slowly as possible into the office, still undecided of what I'm going to do. I suppose the third option is to sleep with her, keep my job and just ensure Alice never finds out. But God, I don't think I could look her in the eye again, knowing I'd cheated on her. She deserves so much better than that. In truth she deserves better than me, but I'm selfish and I want her.

'Tom.' I look up to see her. The dreaded boss smiling at me like I'm the last slice of pizza. 'Can I see you for a moment?' She licks her lips discreetly enough for no-one else to notice but me.

I drag myself unwittingly into her office and quietly shut the door behind me.

She sits herself down behind her desk, shuffling papers like she's busy and about to talk about actual work. A clear power move on her part.

'I've booked a table for us tonight. Eight pm at La Rochealla's and then a room at Premier Inn, so make sure to pack your overnight bag.'

My mouth drops open. How can she just assume that's the decision I've come to? The bitch hasn't even asked me. It gives me the guts to stand up to her, but not before pressing what I hope is record on my phone.

'So, let me get this straight. You want me to sleep with you in order to keep my job? There's no other option?'

She rolls her eyes. 'Tom, I honestly don't know why you keep fighting this. Many men would be honoured to sleep with me. Stop being such a baby.'

'But I have a girlfriend. Isn't there another option?'

'Yes,' she snaps. 'The other option is that you find another job.'

I hope to God it's recorded that.

'You know what? Stuff your job. I don't care if you badmouth me. I'd rather that than sleep with you, you old whore.'

'How dare you!' she shouts, standing up, her face contorted in rage.

'No! How dare you?' I snap back. 'This is sexual harassment and I intend to take it further.'

She sits back down and laughs. 'Good luck there, Tommy boy. My record here is pristine clean. Besides, who's going to believe that little old me sexually harassed the huge hunk? I don't think so.'

She's right.

'Whatever. I'm out of here. I quit.'

I open the door and slam it behind me. Fuck her and fuck this job. Everyone in the open plan office turns to stare at me.

I head straight to the HR department and stroll into the main woman's office.

'Mr Maddens,' she says, taken aback. 'Hi. What can I help you with?'

I press play on my voice recording. Her mouth drops open as she listens to boss bitch confess all.

'Oh my goodness.' she shrieks.

'Tell me she'll be fired?' I beg.

'Well,' she hesitates, 'there will have to be an investigation.'

'Don't fob me off,' I bark. 'Do you think this is enough to have her fired or not?'

She grimaces. 'She'll definitely get a written formal warning, possibly a suspension, but...'

'But with her having been here so long its most probable she'll be back?' I finish for her.

She doesn't have to say anything. Her face says it all.

Alice

A friend I went to uni with passed on my details to a small up and coming jewellery company, so I'm scheduled to do their whole catalogue shoot. It just proves that sending all of those cringey networking emails on Facebook does work sometimes.

I'm just about to leave for the shoot when my phone rings. It's an unknown local number so I answer it cautiously.

'Hello?'

'Hi, can I speak to Alice Watts?'

I clear my throat. 'Speaking.'

'Hi, this is the family planning clinic. I've got the results of your recent STI check.'

'Oh...' I say, my voice clearly strangled. With everything, I'd actually forgotten I was waiting for my results.

'I'm afraid to inform you that your tests came back positive for Chlamydia.'

My mouth drops open and I nearly drop the phone.

'WHAT? Sorry, is this a joke? Has Brooke put you up to this?'

There's a pause at the end of the line. I wait for the person to burst out laughing.

'No, I'm afraid this is really the clinic. If you could please arrange to come in as soon as possible so we can sort you out with some antibiotics. We'll also need you to contact all sexual partners you've had unprotected sex with.'

Oh my god. He's given me a disease. The man I'm supposed to trust most in the world.

Just then the front door opens and in walks Tom.

'It's only fucking one,' I say coldly down the phone, staring at him.

I hang up the phone, more furious than I've ever been in my life. The dickhead lied to me. He said he was clean. I've got fucking Chlamydia because of him! I feel violated.

He stares back at me, his eyes heavy with some kind of emotion. Maybe he got tested too, and he's waiting to tell me.

'I cannot fucking believe you!' I scream, throwing my phone at him.

He ducks out of the way causing it to smash against the wall. 'What the fuck are you talking about?'

'You lied to me!'

His face falls. That's when I realise he already knows. The bastard already knows he gave me a disease.

'You weren't supposed to find out.' He runs his hand down his face. 'It doesn't mean anything.'

'I cannot believe you! Everything we have is based on a total lie.'

He sighs. 'Alice, it was a stupid bet between two idiots. I didn't realise I was going to actually fall for you.'

I frown. Bet? What's he going on about?

'You've lost me?'

He purses his lips, his chin wrinkling. 'Wait, you mean… you don't know about the bet?'

'What bet?' That's when it all falls into place in my mind. He made a bet with one of the boys. A bet that he'd get into my bed. This whole time he's just been trying to get into my pants.

'Wait, if you're not shouting about the bet, what are you shouting at?' he asks.

'You gave me fucking Chlamydia!' I scream. 'You said you'd been tested. You absolute bastard!' I cry, bursting into tears.

He comes closer and tries to hold my arms down, clearly scared of another attack. I struggle against him.

'Are you for real?' he asks, his eyes weary.

'Yes, you fucker!' I smack him on his chest. 'I trusted you and you gave me a fucking disease! I don't even know if this will affect me long term.'

Shit, isn't there one that stops you having babies in the future? Is that Chlamydia?

'Alice...' he looks around, dragging his hand through his hair. 'I... I don't know what to say.'

I take a deep breath, a barrage of traitorous tears running down my cheek. Why am I crying? I'm not upset, I'm pissed off.

'You don't have to say anything, Tom. God knows I wouldn't believe a thing you tell me now.'

He looks down at the floor, all fight in him gone. That's it. He's given up on us.

'I want you to move out.'

He nods, already resigned to my suggestion. What? Not even one little fight for our relationship?

'For what it's worth,' he says, locking broken eyes with me, 'I'm sorry.'

Then he turns and leaves. Just like that, we're over.

Tom

The drive home to Peterborough is rough. Being left

alone with just my thoughts is dangerous right now. I've lost her; the one girl in this world that I'm actually capable of loving. I was going to lose her anyway, but now I've never got a chance of winning her back. No distant possibility somewhere in the future of us finding each other again.

I gave her an STD for fuck's sake. I'm such a dick. Why did I have to lie about being tested? I mean, I have been tested, but... well, when I think about it that's probably about four women ago. Shit. I guess I figured I'd used condoms. I mean, when I think about it it's kind of hard to remember. With some of them I was so wasted it's all kind of blurry, but I've always used condoms. It's just second nature to me.

I'll have to get tested as soon as I get home, even though I'm sure I have it. Shit, I'll have to call all of the women and tell them to get tested too. God, that's humiliating.

Another call from Mum flashes up on my phone. I divert it to voicemail again. Her and Jack have been calling me the last half hour. Alice obviously told Erica which means that Jack knows. He must have rung my mum trying to get hold of me and now she's all worried. Just what I need.

I finally pull into our road and park up on the drive. I take a deep breath, leaning my head against the steering wheel. I need to brace myself for my dad. I'm hoping he's at work, so I have a few hours to come up with something plausible. Some reason why I'm back with no job, just like he predicted.

I drag myself out of the car and walk towards the door.

'Tom!' I turn to see my next-door neighbour Geoff. 'They're already at the hospital.'

I stare back at him. Has he developed dementia since I've been gone? What the hell is he talking about?

I frown back at him. 'Sorry? Who's at the hospital?'

'Your mum and dad,' he answers, as if I'm the crazy one.

'Why, who's sick? Is it my nan?' Shit, I knew I should have visited her more. The woman's in her eighties. She's not going to live forever.

His face visibly pales in front of me. 'Oh, Tom. Do you not know?'

'Know what?' I squawk, my voice breaking from the panic. 'You better tell me quickly what the hell is going on or I'm going to lose it. I've already had the day from hell.'

'It's not going to get any better,' he says with a sad smile. 'It's your dad. He was rushed off in an ambulance. Suspected stroke.'

Fuck. And just like that, when you think your life has already hit rock bottom it goes and shows you there's a basement.

***

Alice

I call Erica, crying down the phone. Apparently so badly that she decided to tell work there had been an emergency. I walked to her flat, needing the fresh air. It only stung my teary eyes. I can't believe this has happened. It's all my own stupid fault for falling for a manwhore like Tom.

She's opening her door when I arrive. She spots me and her face falls.

'Oh, babe. Come here.'

I shamelessly run into her arms and sob onto her

shoulder. My breath is hitched, and snot is running down into my mouth. I've never cried this hard before.

'Come on, take a breath. I'll put the kettle on and you can tell me all about it.'

Well to say Erica is a calming influence is an understatement. She managed to calm me down enough I could relay the whole story. Then she took me back to the clinic to talk through everything with the nurse. I've got antibiotics, and they told me that although Chlamydia can affect future fertility, the fact that I've caught it so quickly stands in my favour. I should hopefully be fine. Tom will have to call all of the girls he's slept with though. I wouldn't want to be receiving that phone call.

We've just got back to my flat after collecting Pickles, when Erica's phone rings. Her face lights up. Must be Jack. She only has that reaction for him.

'Hey, babe,' she says into the phone. 'I'm just getting Alice settled and then I'll be home.'

Great. That means she's already told him about my Tom drama. Her face suddenly pales as she listens to whatever he's saying.

'Shit.'

'What is it?' I whisper, trying to get close enough to hear him.

She turns away from me. 'Okay, I'll tell her. Okay.' She closes the call and turns to me, fidgeting with her necklace. 'Its bad news, Alice.'

'Right...' I stare at her, pleading with my eyes for her to just get it over and done with. 'What's happened?'

'It's Tom's dad. He's died.'

My entire body prickles with cold; goose-pimples

appearing on my arms. I sink down, my legs suddenly like jelly. Tom's dad... dead? This can't be happening.

'Are you sure?' I know it's a stupid question, but it's all I can think of right now.

'I'm sure,' she nods. 'Jack's mum rang.'

'I... I can't believe it,' I stammer. 'How's Tom?'

She bites her lip. 'He doesn't know. He's been trying to call him all afternoon, but he's not answering. Nicholas and Charlie are going to try to find him. Jack's driving up there now.'

'Shit.' I can't even imagine how devastated Tom will be. I know they never got on great, but he's still his Dad. Was he civil the last time he spoke to him? Did they argue? Did he tell him he loved him? God, we're too young to be losing parents.

'Apparently it was a stroke. There we were, all worried about Nic's dad having another heart attack and then this happens.'

'Yeah, I bet it's scared the shit out of him.' I need Tom to know I'm thinking of him. 'Would it be weird for me to text him?'

Erica smiles sadly. 'I don't think it'll hurt.'

'This doesn't mean I forgive him,' I clarify, already unlocking my phone. 'I know it's awful, but I just... I can't take him back just because of this.'

'Alice, that doesn't make you a monster. He gave you an STD. You have every right to still be angry at him. Its's possible to be angry and sad at the same time.'

I get my phone out and send a message.

Tom, I'm so sorry to hear about your dad. Thinking of you x

My phone starts ringing almost immediately. I look down at it, sure it'll be Tom, but it's not.

'Hello?' I answer cautiously.

'Hi, have I reached an Alice Watts?'

'Speaking,' I confirm in my poshest telephone voice.

'Alice, this is Veronica from Glamour magazine. Our photographer for this month's fashion shoot has come down with the flu. We tried to get our fill in photographer Karen Clarke, but she's on holiday. She recommended you.'

'You're joking,' I blurt out. 'I mean... really? Are you serious?'

'I am,' she says. 'But the shoot is Wednesday 5th December. Are you available?'

Am I available? I'd chew off my arm to attend.

'Yes, I'm free that day,' I answer coolly.

She takes my email address and promises to send all the details over later tonight. I can't believe it! My bad case of networking has actually worked! I've got a job at a fashion magazine. This could be the start of my career. The career I actually want.

I accept the job later that night not knowing it would prove to be the date of Tom's dad's funeral.

Chapter 26

Tom

The last week or so has been the worst of my life. When I got to the hospital and found Mum crumpled onto the floor crying hysterically, I knew it was bad. However, I still didn't expect to be told by a doctor that Dad had passed.

I was thinking of all the things I was going to say to him. How I was going to tell him I loved him, and I was sorry for yelling the last time we spoke. So, to be told that I could never tell him... well, it gutted me.

I had to be the strong one as Mum was in bits. First, I called my brother George, who works in London, and told him to come home. I'd wanted to wait until he was here to find out the news, but he sensed in my voice something had happened. I was forced to utter those few tragic words. Dad has died. George broke down on the phone. I still couldn't shed a tear. I had Mum with me.

Since George arrived, he's taken over with making the funeral arrangements. He's always been the organised, in control one. But with nothing to do I've been left helping

Mum understand what's happened. Hell, I don't even understand it myself.

How someone can be here, healthy one minute, and then gone the next? It's just... I don't know, it's all so final. To think I'll never see him again, it's just too much to comprehend.

If I'd have known it was the last time I'd seen him, I would have studied his face more, indented his features into my memory. I would have taken a hundred pictures of the mole he had under his left eye, the wrinkle he gets in between his eyebrows whenever he's lecturing me on how to live my life. God, what I wouldn't give to hear a lecture right now.

Today is finally the funeral. I feel like we've been working towards it for months, not weeks. We arrive in the hired funeral cars behind the hearse. I squeeze Mum's hand before opening the door and getting out. Everyone is crowded silently around the hearse as the funeral directors get the coffin out. Looking on with pity. Just looking at it, knowing my dad is in there, it gets my throat clogging up.

'Are you ready?' the funeral director asks us. He means to carry the coffin. I hand Mum over to Auntie Janice who links arms with her.

I stand forward towards the coffin with George, Uncle Barry, Jack, and Dad's friends Mack and Jason. We're instructed how to lift the coffin and are helped as it's hoisted over our heads and rested onto our shoulders.

Knowing the weight on my shoulders is my dad's body is enough to get my eyes stinging. I blink rapidly until the tears are able to force themselves out. I look to Jack and he's already bawling, his shoulders bouncing up and down so hard I worry we'll drop the thing.

We start the slow walk into the church as *Sailing* by Rod Stewart plays over the speakers. Hearing that raspy bastard's voice talking about flying free above clouds has my chest constricting so tight I have to take deep breaths. It's like this song was written for him.

For as long as I can remember Dad's been obsessed with sailing. Whenever we'd go on holiday he'd find somewhere he could go sailing for the day. My grandad taught him when he was younger. He offered to teach me, but I wasn't interested; the selfish bastard that I am.

I remember asking him once why he never bought a boat of his own. He'd laughed and said they were expensive things. Looking back, I now see what he spent his money on. He invested it in me and George. All of those football lessons, guitar practise, extra tutoring. None of it was free. No wonder he resented me so much for being such a fuck-up.

I force myself to look forward at the empty church. My dad wasn't even religious. God knows why Mum wanted a Church of England funeral. But I suppose they did get married here. Just thinking of her pain has the tears pouring out of my eyes and down my cheeks.

I sniff, praying for my eyes to quickly recover. My Mum can't see me upset. It doesn't work.

We manage to place the coffin down onto the stand at the front of the church with the help of the undertakers. The priest says something to us, but I'm not listening. I'm too busy trying to hold it together as his friends and family take their seats. People are already having to stand at the back. He was so popular. Why didn't I see how great he was while he was alive?

I make my way into the reserved pew and force myself to zone out. If I think of the words being spoken or listen to the sniffs of everyone around me I know I'll break, and I don't want to do that in public. I'll wait until tonight when I can sleep in my own bed and let the unrelenting grief take over. I know once I let it loose, there'll be no going back.

Before I know what's happening, we've taken his body to the crematorium and said goodbye. When we walk out everyone surrounds us with 'I'm sorry' and 'thinking of you,' but the only person I want to talk to is Alice.

I'm in so much pain. From the fact that I'm never going to see my dad again, and also that although I'll see Alice, she'll never be mine—the one person who could have helped me get through this.

The reception is lovely. Or do you call it a wake? God knows. I should really scrub up on my funeral etiquette. We've held it in a local golf club that Dad once joked he'd like his funeral at.

The walls have been decorated with pictures of Dad. It's interesting to see the kind of life he led before he settled down with my mum. He seemed just like me when he was in his twenties. Every picture is of him and a group of mates, all with the same terrible porn star style moustaches. But it's clear that when he met Mum things changed for him. The photos showed how much he adored her. Every single one had him looking on fondly at her. I know myself that you can't fake that kind of adoration in pictures.

My brother George and I were such cute kids although we couldn't have been more different. George has dark brown hair and matching eyes, compared with my blonde hair and green eyes.

I walk over to our table where the gang is still munching on the buffet, and drinking cups of tea. I bring George with me, wanting to introduce him to the girls.

'Hey, guys,' I say, trying to sound chipper and failing. 'You know my brother George, right?'

I see the girls' eyes light up the moment they take him in. I suppose to anyone else he is good-looking. He has some sort of air about him too; I think it's confidence. Not cockiness like me. You just know that he has his shit together. It helps that he's always wearing a suit that fits him like a glove. He pulls out a chair and sits down.

'Hi. Hope you don't mind if I hide here a while. Aunt Carol is on the rounds and she likes to kiss on the lips.' He squirms with a grimace making the girls giggle. 'So, my brother was rude and didn't introduce me to any of you ladies. What are your names?'

I roll my eyes.

He turns to Evelyn first who's busy texting on her phone. No doubt to Omar. She looks up, surprised he's shown any interest in her.

'Well?' he asks with a grin. 'What's your name?'

'Err... Evelyn,' she answers cautiously. It's a first for her to be stuck for words.

He seems to enjoy making her visibly squirm in her seat.

Erica goes around the rest of them introducing each one by one, but he doesn't seem to be able to take his eyes off Evelyn. What's going on here?

'And where is Alice?' he asks them.

My mouth drops open. How would he know anything about Alice? I haven't mentioned anything?

Erica grimaces. 'Alice couldn't make it today.'

I already knew she wouldn't with how we ended things.

'She had her dream job offered to her. It was too good to turn down. Otherwise she'd definitely be here.' She looks at me apologetically.

Dream job? This is the first I've heard of it. But then

it's probably an excuse. I wouldn't put it past Erica to make something up to cushion the blow a bit.

George nods, his eyes shifting in sadness. 'To be brutally honest, I'm tired of being sad today. People are starting to leave, and right now all I want to do is forget for a while and get completely shit-faced.'

Wow. Way to be honest, George.

'So...' Jack says, clapping his hands together, 'who wants shots?'

I'm glad when the last set of people leave the reception. George had to be carried home by our next-door-neighbour an hour ago. Why he thought shots were a good idea, I don't know.

I find Mum taking down the posters, her face a mix of melancholy emotions.

'You okay, Mum?' I ask carefully, helping her to put them away.

'It just wasn't his time, love,' she says with a sad smile. 'He was taken too soon.'

I wrap my arm around her. 'I know, Mum. I know.'

I think back to the last time I talked to him. How we rowed. It's true what they say; never leave loved ones on an argument.

'At least he knew you loved him. The last time I spoke to him I was a dick, and he was thinking what a let-down of a son I am.'

She frowns. 'Your dad loved you.'

I scoff. 'Yeah, right. All I ever caused that man was heartache and stress. Hell, I probably caused this stroke with all of the worry.'

Her eyes turn hard. 'Don't you dare think that. He was immensely proud of you.'

I roll my eyes.

'I mean it, Tom. He was only ever so hard on you because he knew you had so much potential.'

'Potential I've never lived up to, unlike golden balls George.'

She shakes her head. 'George and you are very different, but don't for a minute think that we love you both any differently. Do you know why your dad was so proud of you?'

I shake my head, not believing a word.

'Because you'd managed to move to a different area, get a job, a place to live, and most importantly, you'd found someone to love.'

Alice.

'But he only ever met her once? And I never told you guys we were together.'

She smiles. 'It was enough to see that you were crazy about her. Me and your dad, we were so happy. That's all we ever wanted for you. For you to settle down and be happy with someone you wanted to share your life with. I overheard him telling George about her over the phone.'

Ah, so that's how he knew her name.

I sigh. 'Well, I've fucked that up now, haven't I?'

She smiles sadly. 'What's happened between you two?'

'I fucked up, Mum. Lied to her. Gave her... I did, I did something unforgiveable.'

'Nothing is unforgiveable, Tom.'

God, she really has no idea how much of a fuck-up I am.

'You might think it is, but there's always hope of forgiveness. You don't have any power over whether she chooses to forgive you or not, but you can try to fight for it.'

I put my hands through my hair. 'I don't know, Mum. It's pretty bad.'

She puts her hand on my shoulder. 'Did you know that your dad cheated on me when we first got together?'

My mouth hangs open. Dad cheated on Mum?

'Please tell me you're joking?' I demand, wanting to pummel something.

Why on earth would she tell me that? Taint my memory of Dad so now whenever I think of him I'll get angry at what a cheating bastard he is.

'We were only just together. Things weren't that serious. But yes, he was with that whore Marian from the Old Bell.'

Now I know why she said she had the worst Yorkshire puddings in Peterborough.

'Anyway, your dad confessed everything to me. I was shocked and upset, but I chose to forgive him. And thank God I did. We wouldn't have had all those years together, or you two boys. Those memories that are going to keep me going now he's gone.'

Shit. I can't get my head around this. It's too much to take in at once.

'I can see you're appalled, but don't you see? It just proves that even when someone has done the worst thing imaginable to someone, there's always still hope.'

I sigh, sitting down on one of the chairs. 'So, what do you think I should do?'

'Simple. Fight for her.'

Fight for her. She makes it all sound so easy.

'How?'

'God, you kids of today have no imagination. Alice is

an old-fashioned girl at heart. Romance her. Court her like your father did me.'

'I just don't know if I'm good enough for her, Mum.' I look down at the tablecloth full of coffee stains, not wanting to see the disappointment in her eyes.

'You listen to me.' She takes my chin and forces me to look up at her. 'You *are* good enough for her. You just need to prove it. I know you can do it, baby. You just need some faith in yourself. Luckily, I have enough faith for both of us.'

My phone starts ringing. I look down to see that it's work calling. What the hell do they want?

'Hello?'

'Hi Tom, this is Greg.' Greg is a good guy from my department. He's been there the longest.

'Hi, Greg. Everything okay?' I don't even know if they've heard about my dad.

'Great actually. I thought you'd like to know that the bitch from the east has gone.'

'Huh?' Is he talking about Bernice Shuttlecock?

'That's right. HR asked around after they heard your recording. A few men, including me, admitted to her sexually harassing us. She's been fired, and I've taken on the position.'

'Wow, congratulations.'

'And I want you back, Tom. You're one of our best sales guys. Look, I know you're going through a tough time right now, but I really need you back on Monday. Do you think you could make that happen?'

I look to Mum who's been listening in.

'Of course,' she says with a smile.

'Yeah, okay. I'll see you Monday.'

Chapter 27

Alice

I wake up to banging on the door. I wait for Pickles to start barking, but then I remember she's not here anymore. That I'm all alone. I got in so late last night after the Glamour shoot that I skipped dinner and went straight to bed in my make-up.

I drag myself begrudgingly out of bed passing Tom's empty room. I should really put it up for let, but something's stopping me. Some tiny pathetic hope inside me that Tom will come back. That he'll fight for us. It's so stupid of me. I know he's got more important things on his mind, but I still can't help but hope.

I answer the door, rubbing the sleep out of my eyes.

'Alice Watts?' a guy in a red hat with a clipboard asks.

'Yeah...?' I answer dubiously. He nods to someone behind him, then moves to the side so that another guy holding pots full of violas comes in. He walks right through and along the hallway. Err... rude! I turn back to complain to the guy at the door but there are another two men coming in with violas too. What the hell is happening here?

233

Another two guys come in with flowers. More violas.

'There must be some kind of mistake,' I say to the main guy with the clipboard.

He shakes his head. 'Nope. Alice Watts from apartment 226b. It says right here.'

'Well, who the hell sent this amount of flowers? There must be a mistake with how many flowers they ordered.'

'I'm afraid that's confidential, Miss.'

God, this guy's a dick. I grab the clipboard off him, but he tries to grab it back. I elbow him in the ribs and he doubles over. Bloody baby.

I quickly look down to the sender details. Tom Maddens. Tom sent these?

'Is there a note?' I ask the clipboard guy a little too desperately.

'Yeah. One of these has it.'

The guys look between each other. 'I thought you had it?' they say to each other.

'Oh Jesus, you're useless.'

I scan down the clipboard again, moving when he tries to snatch it back again.

Note to be included: *Please forgive me.*

'Oh, and I almost forgot this,' the man says reaching into his pocket. He hands over an envelope.

My shaky hands scramble to open it, hoping it's a letter. I pull out some kind of ticket. I read it. 'Brighton vintage fair.' One ticket. How did he know I wanted to go to this? I remember seeing the poster in the toilets at Nicholas' birthday dinner. Did Brooke help him with this? Does he have the other ticket, or did he just buy me one?'

Well, the fair is tomorrow. I guess I'm going to find out.

I look around at all the violas, my flat now smelling irresistibly sweet. I've never told him how much I love violas. Then I remember the day I took him for a picnic near his work. We sat next to some. Can he really be that sweet? Or could it be a coincidence?

My phone rings. I look down at it expecting to see Tom's name flashing back at me. Instead it's a withheld number again.

'Hello?'

'Miss Watts, it's PC Edwards here. I just wanted to give you an update. Is now a good time?'

'Err, yeah that's fine. What's happened?'

'We've got enough evidence to prove that Mr Cundy posted the pornographic picture of you. We've sent it all on to the Crown Prosecution Service. It'll be up to them to decide whether to charge him or not.'

'Wow. Thanks so much for all of your help.'

'There's another thing. We traced the IP address of the emails that were being sent to your friends and family. It turned out to be someone completely different. A Gerald Watts. I'm assuming he's a relative of yours?'

My stomach nearly drops out of my knickers. Gerald? He sent the emails? What a spiteful bastard. I had no idea he hated me that much.

'Yes. He's my brother.'

'Right.'

'Look, is there any way I can drop the charges?' I don't want to take this tool to court. 'Just let him off with a warning?'

'I'll pass it on that you're feeling forgiving but it's up to the CPS now.'

'Ok, well, thanks for everything.'

I can't believe Gerald did that. You hear about these overprotective brothers looking out for their sisters, and there's mine sending around my amateur porn. Sicko.

I take my phone out and type a text message to my mum.

Gerald is in trouble with the police for circulating a naked picture of me. If that doesn't make you realise what a weirdo he is, nothing ever will.

Tom

Phase one of 'Win Back Alice' is complete. I've had a notification from the delivery company that it went through this morning. But... I still haven't heard from her. That was three hours ago and no matter how hard I stare at my phone, she's not tried to contact me. I knew she wasn't going to be an easy nut to crack so I'm moving onto phase two.

I call Jack.

'Hey dude, how are you doing?'

'I've been better,' I admit. 'Anyway, I'm ringing for a favour. Can you get the girls to keep Alice out of the flat the morning of her birthday?'

He yawns. 'Next Wednesday? Yeah, I'm sure I can. Why, what you got planned?'

'Just promise you'll help me first.'

He sighs. 'Okay, fine. I'm in.'

Friday 7th December

Alice

This morning I woke up to an envelope through the post in Tom's handwriting. Inside it was a picture of Tom and

Pickles in the park with a background of violas. Written on the back was *'We miss you'*.

I'm dressed up in my vintage orange coat with faux-fur trimmed collar. Underneath, I'm wearing my vintage 1940's navy and ivory polka-dot wrap-dress. It's always been my 'go to' confident dress. It gives me curves that I don't have and makes me feel both sexy and classy. I've teamed it with matching navy and red heels.

I queue up with what seems like hundreds of people for the vintage fair. I keep looking around, but I can't seem to find Tom. Maybe he did just get me a ticket. I suppose it's not really his thing anyway. He'd probably moan the whole way around. Yes, I'm better on my own. That doesn't stop me doing a double take whenever I see a blonde guy though.

I hand over my ticket to the woman. She pauses when she spots my name.

'Ah, you're Alice.'

'Err.... yeah. Why?' I ask dubiously.

She smiles. 'I'm supposed to give you this.' She hands over a piece of paper.

'Oh, thanks.' I take it and open it frantically as I walk into what looks like a cave of wonders. Dress stalls, workshops on how to do victory rolls, 'high tea for two' cafes. It's like heaven.

Alice,

I bought this ticket for you with no conditions and I hope you enjoy your day. But, in case you'd like to see me, I'll be waiting by the candyfloss stand.

All my love

Tom xxx

Wow. A love letter of sorts. From Tom 'Manwhore' Maddens. I can't believe it. I wander into the first clothes stall and start looking through the dresses, my head still in a bit of a daze. Should I meet up with him? Would it be nicer if I just texted him and said thanks, but I won't have time?

I don't want to give the guy false hope. We can't be together. We just won't work when I don't trust him. Especially with everything that's gone on between us. But the guy has just lost his dad. Maybe I should see him, be friendly at least.

Oh, who am I kidding? I'm walking to find the candyfloss stand before I can talk myself back out of it. I get shoved on the shoulder by someone walking past. We both turn to apologise to the other. That's when I see him. Not Tom, but Ted.

His eyes widen when he realises it's me. 'Shit. Alice…'

'Ted.' I take a deep breath. 'You should be ashamed of what you did to me.'

He hangs his head. 'I know. For what it's worth, I am sorry.'

'Bit late now that the entire world has seen my tits, don't you think?'

He nods, biting on his lip. 'Look, there's something else I need to tell you. I was going to email.'

I fold my arms across my chest. 'What is it, Ted? I don't have time for this.'

'Well…' he takes a deep breath. 'You need to get checked for Chlamydia.'

My mouth drops open. 'Sorry? What?'

'I've just found out I've got Chlamydia. You should get checked too.'

I think back to when we first got together. He'd talked me into us not using a condom. Showed me a report from the local clinic saying he was clean.

'You faked the report?' I can't help but blurt out. 'You

tricked me?'

'No, actually,' he snarks back. 'But, well, I kind of got it while we were dating.'

'Sorry?' I stare back at him, my face blank. What does he mean? He's squirming now. Wait… 'You mean you cheated on me?'

He huffs. 'I didn't mean for it to happen.'

I nod and snort. 'But it did, without a condom, and you didn't think to protect me from anything you might have gotten. Nice, Ted. Real nice. You know I've been blaming someone else for giving me this, when I've actually probably given it to him!'

He scoffs. 'Who, that prick you sent round to see me? Sorry if I don't feel too bad for someone that held me down and threatened to expose my dick to the world.'

'Whatever, Ted. Good luck in your court case. Hopefully I won't ever have to see you again.'

I storm away from him, livid. I just want to see Tom now. I spot him standing next to the candyfloss machine looking anxiously at his phone every few seconds. He's obviously worried I'm not coming.

Seeing Tom like this is enough to break my heart. I want nothing more than to bundle him up and take him away from all of this. Somewhere he can forget it all for a moment. To see the heartbreak in his eyes, God, it just guts me. It's making me wonder if I was right throwing him out at all, even with what I did think.

When someone dies you realise what's important in life. Not that I'm ready to forgive him for everything. Even if I was, I can't be with him. He still started our relationship on a lie. A bet. Once the trust has gone in a relationship there's nothing left. I know that better than most people. I'm just glad I didn't send this one any sexy pictures.

He looks up, as if sensing my presence and spots me, a

smile forming on his lips.

'Alice,' he almost whispers, as if saying a prayer.

'Hi, Tom.' I walk towards him, my hands shoved in my pockets, so I don't fidget. 'How are you?'

'I've been better,' he admits on a shrug.

'I'm so sorry I didn't come to the funeral. Only I couldn't turn down the job.'

He puts his palm up to stop me. 'Alice, I'm glad you took the opportunity. Plus, you really do owe me nothing. Especially after the way we ended things.'

I swallow, avoiding his eyes. 'So... did you want to tell me something? Or were you just looking for a chat?' I tuck my hair behind my ear.

He smiles sadly. 'I just wanted to explain myself a bit.'

I sigh. 'Tom, there's no point. What's done is done. There's no point going over it again.'

'Please, Alice,' he begs, his eyes pleading.

'Fine. What do you want to say?'

He takes a deep breath. 'Look, I handled the whole thing terribly. Obviously, I thought I was clean, but when I think about it now I was tested about four girls ago.'

'Tom, it was me.'

He stares back at me, his brows furrowed. 'What was you?'

I gulp. 'The Chlamydia. I just found out that it was Ted that gave it to me. Which means I probably gave it to you. Did you get tested?'

He nods then pulls me in for a hug. 'It's not your fault, Alice. I don't blame you for assuming badly of me.'

'I... what if I hadn't have gotten tested? This could have stopped me from having children. That's a huge thing for me. I can't believe him.'

'He's a dick.'

I lean back to look into his face. 'You still bet on getting me into bed.'

'I'm sorry.' He looks genuinely gutted. 'You have no idea how bad I feel. I couldn't put it into words if I tried.'

'Well then why didn't you fight for us, Tom?' I can't help but cry. I take a discreet deep breath to try to stop my eyes stinging. 'You gave in and moved out.'

He pulls his hand through his hair. 'Look, I lied to you before about having it all sorted with my boss. I'd just been told that I was basically fired because I turned down her advances and that I'd be bad-mouthed all around Brighton.'

I tut. 'Another lie, Tom. Really?'

He grimaces. 'The way I saw it I'd already messed up any chance of living here, so I thought a clean break while you were angry at me was the best thing to do.'

I shrug. 'Maybe it was.'

He takes my hands, holding me captive with his piercing green eyes. 'I don't expect you to take me back; but know I'm here just in case you ever want to forgive me. I'll be waiting for you.'

'You might be waiting forever,' I admit, looking down at the ground.

'Then I'll wait forever,' he nods, his eyes sincere. 'Here.' He reaches into his jeans pocket and takes out a wrapped-up present. 'This is for you. I bought it before we broke up.'

I go to unwrap it, but he stops me. 'No. Please promise me you won't open it until your birthday morning.'

'Seriously?' I laugh. 'I have to wait?'

'Please,' he nods. 'Just do that one thing for me.'

'Okay.' I nod, take it, and kiss him briefly on his cheek. He closes his eyes. 'Goodbye, Tom.' I turn and walk away.

'Remember, Alice,' he shouts over to me. 'I'll be waiting.'

Chapter 28

Wednesday 12th December

Alice

I wake up depressed. There's no sound of Pickles scurrying around the corner. No sound of Tom's bare feet thudding along the floor. I'm all alone. Happy birthday me. But I have one thing to look forward to. Finally opening the present from Tom.

I rush out into the living room, throwing my dressing gown on along the way. I grab the present and the few posted cards I've had delivered. It's funny, but now I'm allowed to open my gift, I almost want to prolong it. I leave it to one side and instead open one of the cards. The first one is from my parents.

To Alice,

Enjoy your birthday,

Mum, Dad, and Gerald.

Well, that's formal. I'm really feeling the love. Funny how Mum never texted me back the other day and he's still being included on my birthday card. Forgiven him as always then.

The next card is from the zoo. It's actually more lovingly written than the one by my parents.

Okay, now I'm doing it. Opening the present Tom gave me. I rip at the red wrapping paper until a red velvet box is revealed underneath. Jewellery? He's got me jewellery?

I open it up carefully and nearly drop the box. Nestled inside is the brooch I saw and fell in love with that day we were shopping in the lanes. I didn't think he'd even noticed what I'd been looking at.

It's a 1960's large floral gold design that almost looks like violas, only each opening of the flower has a different gemstone. I'd noticed how it had all of us girls' birthstones on it; there's garnet for Erica in January; Peridot for Brooke in August, Emerald for Molly in May and Tanzanite and Turquoise for both me and Evelyn this month.

It's so rare to find all our gemstones in the same shop, let alone in the same brooch. I'm always looking for a necklace with our stones in it, and now I have this brooch from the past which feels like it was made just for me.

I can't believe he went back and got me this. It was over a hundred pounds. Plus, it's not like I was dropping any hints or anything. I just looked at it in passing. I didn't even think he'd noticed. How wrong was I? What else didn't I notice?

My front door suddenly opens and in crash the girls holding balloons, banners, coffee, and a cake box.

'Happy birthday!' they all sing showering me in kisses.

'We have coffee from your favourite coffee shop,' Erica says handing me one.

'And chocolate fudge cake for breakfast from...' Evelyn says with a big grin.

'No!' I choke in shock. 'Not...'

'Yep!' Molly coos. 'From Choccywoccydoodah's! We

know you said you'd love to have one of their cakes for breakfast one day. Well, your birthday wish is our command.'

'God, I love you guys.' I'm always looking in their shop window at all the out-of-this-world cakes.

I open the box to see the most delicious looking chocolate cake in the world. I take a knife from the drawer and cut it up in equal pieces. I pass around the disposable forks —trying to ignore that they're bad for the environment— and break off a bit. I place it in my mouth and let the flavours overwhelm me. Damn, it's chocolate fudge cake.

'Oh my gawd!' I moan through a mouthful. 'This is like heaven.'

'What's that you got there?' Evelyn asks taking my brooch from the side.

'Ooh, that is so adorable!' Brooke says. 'Who got you that?'

I squirm uncomfortably. 'Tom did.'

'What?' Evelyn nearly chokes out. 'When did he give you that?'

I explain about the violas, some of which are still dotted around the flat—the rest I gave to the children's wing at the hospital—the vintage fair tickets, his apology, and now this brooch.

Brooke smiles when I mention the vintage fair. It was definitely her that mentioned it to him.

'Wow,' Evelyn gasps. 'I hate to say it, but he really is trying.'

'He is,' Erica agrees, nodding frantically. 'He's living on our sofa right now.'

'Really? I thought he left his job?'

'They fired that old cow. He's back working there now.'

'Ah, so he just wants his room back then,' I say sadly. 'That makes sense.'

'No, Alice,' Molly says, taking my hand. 'I've seen him. He's in bits without you. Look at everything he's done. Someone doesn't do that just to get a room back in a flat.'

'Anyway,' I say, shaking my head, 'let's talk about something else. My head is all over the place with this.'

'Fine. We're going to a spa!' Molly claps like an excitable seal. 'So, get your stuff and let's go chill out for the day.'

'That sounds bloody perfect.'

Tom

The girls surprised her with a spa day, so it's given me and the boys time to do everything I've wanted. That's how guys deal with loss. We don't talk about it, but we show our mates we're here for each other with action. They all dropped everything to help here all day. And I've really put them to work.

I've been told Alice is on her way home. I've just finished off the vegan curry from her recipe book. It looks... well, it looks *sort of* edible. I've made sure to set the table with an arrangement of the delivered violas, glad she didn't throw them straight in the trash. I hear the door go, my heart beating crazily.

She rounds the corner cautiously. I'm scared shitless of her reaction. She could just go mental and throw me out straightaway. I deliberately didn't bring Pickles. I don't want her to have any bearing over her decision.

She stops dead in her tracks when she sees me, looking with eyes wide for a long time.

'Tom?' she asks.

I smile and rock awkwardly on my heels.

'It's me, yeah.'

We stare at each other again for a few more minutes. I shake myself off trying to get going. 'I've made you a vegan curry. Sit down.'

She smiles kindly and sits down. The worst bit is not knowing if she's just being polite and only doing this because my dad just died. Not because she's even considering forgiving me.

'You really made this yourself?' she asks as she looks over it. 'I'm not gonna find some M&S containers in the bin?'

I chuckle. 'You haven't tasted it yet.'

She picks up a spoon and tastes a bit. I do the same. Shit, this tastes like crap. I see her face contort but she quickly tries to cover it.

'It's okay. It tastes like shit,' I admit on a grin.

She bursts out laughing and spits the rest back into the bowl. We both crease over laughing. I've so missed laughing with her. Doing anything with her really. My soul just feels at ease even being in the same room as her.

'Maybe we should order pizza?' Alice says with a smile.

'Or maybe we should talk first? Get the awkwardness out of the way?'

She swallows. 'Okay. We can talk about the elephant in the room.'

'Okay.' I stand up and walk around the table to sit next to her. I take her hand. 'I want to know if you'll give me another chance. I know I don't deserve it, but just hear me out.'

She looks down at her hand in mine.

'But,' I say quickly, wanting to get my speech out before she has a chance to speak again. 'I don't want you to feel sorry for me because my dad died. I want you to imagine that hasn't happened. I want you to be honest.

'I feel shit about lying to you, but I didn't realise how amazing you were when I made that bet. I never used to value sex. It was just another fuck for me.' She squints, wondering where I'm going with this. 'But that was all until I fell for you. Sex with you is different. Everything is different with you. I feel different when I'm with you. Like I'm worth loving.'

She smiles sadly, her eyes turning glassy.

'But I get that I don't deserve your love. I'm just some fuck boy that hurt you, but please know that version of me is the old Tom. Everything is so much clearer now. I want to make memories with you, just like my mum had with my dad. I want to fill a photo album with all of our firsts. I want to know the day I die that I've spent it with the person I love.'

She inhales sharply. Her eyes close for a second. 'You love me?' she asks disbelievingly.

'How can you doubt that? Of course, I love you.'

'Look, I forgive you, okay. But don't say things you aren't sure about.' She shakes her head. 'I don't need *I love you's.*'

Smiling, I stroke her soft cheek. 'I know, but I do. Fine, if you don't believe me, but you will eventually.'

She smiles. I take my cue to lean in. I hover my hand over her porcelain-pale cheek, grazing my fingers on her perfect lips. She closes her eyes and sighs contentedly. I take that as a sign and lean in, kissing those pretty little lips I've come to love so much.

I break it off quicker than she wants. I know because she follows me when I lean back.

'I've got a surprise for you.'

She grins. 'Better than this curry?'

'It's not hard,' I chuckle. I stand up, pulling her hand so she's forced to stand. Then I lead her to my old bedroom door. 'I hope you like it.' I stand back and let her open the door, a suspicious look on her face.

She walks in, no doubt expecting a red room of pain or something equally as creepy, to instead find her new photography dark room the guys helped me put together. Complete blackout curtains are duct taped around the windows, so all sense of light is taken out. Chemistry trays are set up on my old set of drawers, along with tongs. The red hue from the safelight makes the room have a cosy kind of glow.

'It's not completely ready. We still need to get the chemicals, but it's a start, right?'

She turns around and grabs my face. She slams her lips against mine, pushing her tongue in.

I laugh. 'So, I take it you like?'

'I love.' She beams at me. 'And I love you. Don't get me wrong, I'm still kind of furious with you, but life's too short to let this get in the way.'

'I can't tell you how happy I am you said that, because I can guarantee I'm going to fuck-up again. But I want you to forgive me each time because life without you isn't a life at all.'

She smiles. 'Just don't fuck-up so epically next time, yeah?'

Epilogue

Christmas Day

Alice

Tom's Mum passes over the roast potatoes. It's their first Christmas without Tom's dad and my first one with their family. We've left a chair and place setting for him and placed his framed photo there, so we feel like he's part of it. Tom's family are still far more functional than mine.

Once our food has been laid out, Tom's brother George raises his glass of red wine.

'I'd like to make a toast,' he smiles. 'To Dad. I hope he's looking down on us proud of the lives we're living. I know he'll be proud of you, Tom.'

Tom smiles back sadly. I clasp his hand under the table and give it a reassuring squeeze.

'With the help of Alice, you've actually turned into a top bloke.'

We all laugh. Tom rolls his eyes. 'Yeah, love you too, George.'

'But seriously,' George says smiling at his mum. 'I love you guys, and I hope this new year brings us nothing but joy.'

Damn, that guy can give a speech. I couldn't believe it when I met his brother and found he was even more charming than Tom.

'Too right it will,' Tom says clinking his glass with mine. 'Starting with a trip to Barcelona next month.' Thankfully, the company had let us re-arrange my prize.

I smile back at him. Our relationship might not have a perfect record, but I do truly believe Tom is perfect for me. When you look at us on paper we're opposites, but when you put us together we're forced towards each other like magnets.

If anything, Tom lying, and us contracting a bloody STI forced us to really think about what we wanted. For all we know we might have skirted around the idea of a relationship for a long time and ended up falling out anyway. This way I know he loves me, and I love him.

Is he a risk? Of course he is. But every great reward is always after the biggest risk. And I'm willing to take a leap of faith. For Tom I'd jump off a building as long as he promised to catch me.

THE END

Sign up for Laura's newsletter so you don't miss out on the next Babes of Brighton book – http://eepurl.com/bpR2ar

Also by
LAURA BARNARD

Debt & Doormat Series

The Debt & the Doormat

The Baby & the Bride

Porn Money & Wannabe Mummy

Babes of Brighton Series

Excess Baggage

Love Uncovered

One Month Til I Do Series

Adventurous Proposal

Marrying Mr Valentine

Standalones

Tequila and Tea Bags

Dopey Women

Heath, Cliffs & Wandering Hearts

Road Trip

Sex, Snow & Mistletoe

31093373R00145

Printed in Poland
by Amazon Fulfillment
Poland Sp. z o.o., Wrocław